FINCHES

By A.M. Muffaz

FINCHES

Cover art © 2021 by I. L. Vinkur

Design and interior by ElfElm Publishing

Quote Attribution:

Quran, The Holy Qu-ran, Text, Translation & Commentary by Abdullah Yusuf Ali. Published by Khalil Al-Rawaf 1946: https://quranyusufali.com/about-quranyusufali-com/

The Origin of Species by Charles Darwin, online version here. Original publication info: https://en.wikisource.org/wiki/On_the_Origin_of_Species_(1859)#Contents

Available as a trade paperback and eBook from Vernacular Books.

ISBN: 978-1-952283-16-1

Visit us online at VernacularBooks.com

For Seth, Kris and everyone who believed that I could.

Introduction

I originally began writing *Finches* 15 years ago partly to process, emotionally, how Muslim polygamy affected families—mine and the people around us. It is legal in Malaysia, where I was born and raised, for Muslim men to take up to four simultaneous wives. And while only a very small fraction of Muslims practice plural marriage, it seems like everybody knows someone whose life was touched by this issue. In my experience, polygamy only brings grief to every person it touches. There is all the betrayal of adultery, for wives and their children, with the added dagger of it being a religious duty they must swallow.

This is why I knew when I started writing, one of the conceits I wanted to include was to name the women after the most important women in Muhammad's, the prophet of Islam's, life. It was important to explore how the dynamics of the Islam's first family has tainted the marriage of every Muslim thereafter. Thus, Grandmother Jah (a diminutive of

Khatijah) is named after Muhammad's first wife, Khadijah, a woman it is said he respected so highly, he did not take any other wife during her lifetime.

Fatimah was the name of Muhammad's sole surviving child with Khadijah, and the only child to survive his death. Like her mother, he cherished Fatimah so highly he forbade her husband from marrying anyone else while she lived. Finally, there is Aisya, named after Aisha, Muhammad's youngest wife and the only virgin he married. His undisputed favourite, she was the second of his plural wives, living her whole life born into and in the service of Islam.

Then and now, marriage among Muslims is regarded as a pillar of Islamic life. This is reflected by Ghani's aspirations for his son, Rahim—whose name is also the Malaysian language word for "womb". Incidentally, Habib means "beloved", a hint as to his true position within the story.

Power between Muslim men and women are inevitably skewed towards patriarchy. Imagine for a moment a husband promising to love and honour his wife for their entire lives together, but with the caveat that if the husband chooses to do so, he may take further partners for himself. Consent is a fraught concept in this situation. In Malaysia, when a man takes a second wife or divorces a wife, people blame the first wife for not being good enough. This is a cultural landscape where the appearance of harmony is more important than its reality. The shame of being inadequate was something I wanted each member of Ghani's family to experience differently. Whether they take it to the chin or fight it utterly, transmute that disappointment into a bitterness—each person's reaction forms a story within a story, my reason for shaping the book as vignettes.

In *Finches*, it is Grandmother Jah who chooses to stay married but separated from Ghani. Her insistence is predicated on leaving her children an inheritance, rather than losing it all with a divorce. It is no coincidence that Fatimah's daughter is named after her mother—I used it to solidify Grandmother Jah's position as the "correct" relationship and Aisya's role as that of an outsider, an aberration that shouldn't be there. What was the real relationship between the original Fatimah and her husband's youngest wife—probably younger than herself when they married? Interpretations vary, but I would imagine it never stops feeling unnatural to treat someone your own age as your mother.

Given how long it took me to finish this book, that first exploration of polygamy's effects eventually became a way for me to process a different trauma, the realisation that the flawed, beautiful, colourful and diverse country I remember from my childhood has only grown more alien to me the older I get. Coming from a place where the politics are poisonous should be familiar to many of my readers here in America. The difference is that people here are more willing to loudly fight against the insidious puritanism and bombastic religiosity, to say something about institutional racism. It's not nice to think critically in my culture. Gentleness—the state of being quietly accepting and only quietly changing the world around you—is the ideal where I come from. So here is a book that is quietly being loud.

The relationship between Loong and Khatijah, a Chinese person and Malay one, reflects a more modern perspective of how things can be. There is a personal reason too why I would include this. As a child of a mixed-race marriage myself, I have seen first-hand the deep racial mistrust underneath my country's obsession with harmony. Growing up, the question I got most was whether I was Malay or Chinese. When I was little, I relished in seeing the shock on people's faces at my answer. As I grew older, it began to irk me people would even ask. Eventually, my answer to their question was always just, "I'm Malaysian." I see normalising mixed-race relationships as one of the most important tools we have for normalising cultural understanding. No government dicta is as powerful as a mixed-race family's lived reality.

Living authentically is, unfortunately, a distant dream for anyone Malaysian culture labels an "other". Rahim's relationship in my story is one of these "others". Malaysian law, secular and religious, criminalises sodomy and oral sex as jailable offences. The subtlety of Rahim and Habib's interactions are underscored by the idea that what they are doing is illegal. My goal with writing Rahim's POV was primarily to depict a normal man experiencing the loss of his father, whom like many children the world over, loves and disappoints his parents. These are people, who like you and I, struggle with work, experience romance, deal with grief and have siblings they get along or spar with. Who they love should not be criminal. Finding the right person who supports you, cares for you and willingly shares all of life's experiences together with you is hard enough as it is. We should always treat it as a rare blessing.

As for why I named this book *Finches*: When Charles Darwin set out on his famous visit to the Galapagos Islands in 1835, he collected finch specimens that showed unusual variations in beak structure across different islands. He eventually realised each different beak was adapted to the specific conditions of each island, which critically informed his theory of natural selection. Variation and adaptation are things that haunt, even horrify, many of the key characters in my book. Put differently, their fear of change was worse than the change itself. It's a lesson worth remembering.

Darwin originally aspired to be a parson when he boarded the HMS *Beagle*, as closed and content an existence as could be. At the end of it, the life-changing revelations he came to would challenge generations of people to see change as beautiful. Perhaps to some extent, *Finches* will help you see that too.

Ghani's Family Tree

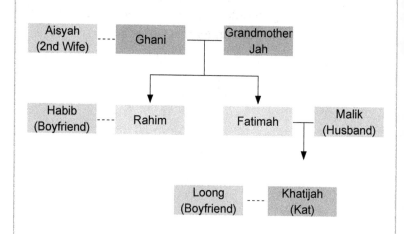

Jah

"And be not like the woman who breaks into untwisted strands, the yarn she has spun after it has become strong."

—*Surah Al Nahl, Ayat 92*

———

WHEN GRANDMOTHER JAH CROSSED THE THRESHOLD OF the house, the very timbers creaked in obeisance. She could feel the cold in the tiles waft up through her feet, igniting every joint in her body.

She'd draped a shawl over her head, which over the course of the day had fallen completely to her shoulders. She picked it off to wipe the sweat around her neck. The sheer gauze quickly soaked through.

Khatijah had her hands in a firm grip around her arm. As she helped her grandmother to the sofa, she mumbled encouraging words, like, "Just a little more," and "We're getting closer."

Grandmother Jah waved her away with folds of her sweat-stained, perfume-scented shawl. "I'm not an invalid. Go see if you can get me some water."

She flattened her feet against the tiles, which seemed to have grown increasingly cold. The floor tiles were chipped. The scuffs scratched her soles. They had been green when she married Ghani. Now they were the colour of faded mould.

From the open doorway, she could also see the garden, which had been wholly her husband's effort. When she'd seen it last, it was a thriving vegetable garden, set beneath a mango orchard as tall as her son was old. Rahim had the mango trees chopped down, so across a meadow of moss and ant trails there were only stumps, like seats for trolls. Worn pavers traced old paths between the beds. From her view, they were like grave markers. She remembered a time when her children practised writing their names on them with sticks and water.

Bougainvilleas were halted at their embankments, the crudely cut branches stark against the otherwise thriving foliage. Among their thorns she saw the borders of her home, and within their bounds, an immediate distance from all other things.

Inside, Ghani hadn't changed so much as a nail, not even the plywood thresholds that had stood against all twenty-seven years of floods and children. The plasticine used to stop the gaps between the door frame and the walls was dark with dirt. If the next monsoon rose above the drains, the splintered plywood would be of little help.

Khatijah returned with water in a teacup.

Grandmother Jah recognised the teacup: stoneware from

her aunt on the occasion of her marriage, the lacquer etched with fine cracks and the bottom ringed with stains. Jah's skin was as yellow as the handle around which she hooked her finger. Her palms, worn from years of squeezing tamarind fruits, were tarnished like month-old henna. She said, "I wonder if I'll live long enough to see your hand coloured in henna. It probably won't be long."

Khatijah laughed and put her sunburnt hand in hers. "Don't say things like that. You'll outlive us all."

"Don't let the devils hear you. I'm old. I'll live to see my grandchildren grow up."

"And I have college to finish, and work to do. It'll be a long time before I think of anything else." Khatijah glanced at the men in the driveway. "I'll go see if they need help."

Grandmother Jah sipped her water and smiled.

She watched her son, his boyfriend and her granddaughter's boyfriend unload her things from the car. The front doors were bordered with iron grilles that safeguarded the home like a jail. The wood on the doors was cracked in three layers: green, orange and a kind of muddy brown she hadn't seen since Rahim was five. With the doors thrown open, they could see clear across the driveway to the street and the brush beyond. It was still a small village, even with the city creeping up around it on all sides. The familiarity chafed.

A house lizard crawled out of its hole in the wall.

Outside, sunspots lit the concrete behind Rahim's feet. Rahim had pale soles and coffee-coloured skin up to his ankles. They were like his father's feet, about the size of his father's shoes. Whenever the light shivered behind his legs, she saw an identical set of feet, like a mirror image caused by her wavering eyesight—an image that lacked a body. But wherever her son walked, his heels would brush this other man's toes.

The house lizard cackled.

——

"I'll call you when I reach Perth." Rahim leaned in to peck her on the cheek.

Grandmother Jah wrapped her thick arms around her son's shoulders. He had a boy's shoulders, bony and square. "Take care."

With his breath still warm on her face, he pulled away. It made her heart break, but she opened her eyes to watch him go. Habib, her son's companion, grasped her fingertips weakly, like a gentleman to a stranger. She reached around to grasp his fingers firmly in her hands. He had a nice smile.

"You take care too," said Loong. The boy Khatijah had chosen was swarthy and short, with hair shaved far too close to his head, but his hands were warm, readily enclosing hers. He kissed her knuckles with cracked lips, even though he didn't have to, even though this mark of respect was notably un-Chinese. Grandmother Jah considered him a sweet boy.

Khatijah kissed her knuckles and gave her a hug. Grandmother Jah patted her granddaughter's head, full of hair like short ripples packed tight against her scalp, much like her own. Her eyes were large and clear, dancing with life above her dimpled cheeks. No trace of Ghani existed on this child's face. Further down the line, she knew, he would cease to be remembered completely.

"If you need anything, give us a call." Khatijah withdrew in a whisper of polyester. "If you want me to pick up some groceries after school, just let me know."

"I know how to use a taxi."

"Just in case." Khatijah chuckled. "You know my number."

"I do."

They left, Habib and Khatijah waving from the back seat, with Rahim smiling from the front.

Grandmother Jah put on the evening news and went to put the kettle to boil. She peeked into the fridge for the dinner Khatijah left behind. There were fresh groceries too. Basic greens in the crisper and cuts of chicken in the freezer. Some rice and soy sauce were left over from the previous occupants. Grandmother Jah would have thrown them away, but it was a sin to throw away food.

Rahim had gotten her a microwave oven, which she used to heat up the biryani her granddaughter had bought. There hadn't been a matching set of crockery in this house since she married her husband, and there certainly wasn't one left over after his death. She used the plainest of the lot to warm her food, hoping that a plate that predated coloured television was safe enough for the modern world.

Coffee jars lined the lowest shelf above the counter, powdered with dust and sealed with grease. Through the glass, she could make out lumps of cabbage, trapped like viscera adrift in yellowed brine. Shaking a jar roused a milky louche that stirred, like a curl of dragon, from the debris at the bottom. A Chinese neighbour had taught her the process: First, the cabbage leaves had to be wilted in the sun for a day. Then they were rubbed with salt before they were packed in jars under a mixture of water and rice flour. The leaves would express their own brine in time, adding a sourness more pleasant than vinegar.

By two weeks, the whites would wash out, retaining a hint of green at the tips. By two years, the colour would be leached clear off the veins, and the hearts would take on the translucence of matured ivory.

Unscrewing the lid of a jar released its perfume, sour with a hint of sea water. Grandmother Jah reached for a leaf and bit into it, noting with satisfaction that it was tender and still good. Bringing the remainder to the chopping board, she tested her cleaver on the edge of a stem. The blade bent the fibres without breaking the skin.

The pickles were as old as the day she'd left her husband, and her cleaver, she knew, was as dull as the brine was sharp. It was a shame to let blades dull, a shame on the woman in whose care the kitchen had fallen. Grandmother Jah nodded to herself as she reached for the sharpener beneath the sink. Spider webs clung in tendrils to her hand as she withdrew it from behind the sponges, the sharpening wheel a comforting weight in her grip.

Lifting her skirt to slightly below her knees, with only her soles to support her, she collapsed herself into a squat. Her bones ached at the effort, but the first brush of the blade against the whetstone made a sound like the pull of a yo-yo's string, a pleasure that brought a smile to her lips. As she whirred her wheel upon the floor, the grooves on the outer ring bumped against the floor tiles, tapping a beat. From a crack in the wall came the patter of a house lizard, laughing to its friends in the ceiling. Gristle began to rise across the edge of the blade, exuding its mineral scent, like salt and iron.

Behind her back, the floorboards in the hallway began to creak, sure, heavy treads spaced a footstep apart. They stopped, she surmised, where the kitchen doorway began. The boards groaned as though the person there shifted his weight, as though he turned to look through the door.

Grandmother Jah steadied her wrist with her free hand, frowning as she slowed the path of the wheel to match her breathing. She counted a single inhalation for a single roll forward, and a single exhalation for every single roll back. Five breaths passed in this way before the floorboards began their noise once more. The footsteps headed down the hall, pausing, she calculated, at the entrance to the master bedroom. Two more breaths passed, the second halted halfway, before she was able to stop, resting the tip of the cleaver upon the floor.

She turned to her left, looking directly at the wall beside her, and raised her voice. "This is my house," she said, with a slight waver, and then, "I live here now," like the point of the blade she aimed at the ground.

There were no more footsteps for many more breaths. Her mettle and her confidence in her knees restored, she inched her way upright, the cleaver and the wheel with her. She ran the cleaver under the tap, letting the water slap against the sink. When the water ran clear, she shut it off, shaking the droplets away from the knife even as she brought it back to the board. The cabbage leaf sliced cleanly with a swish.

The mattress was a thick slab of foam that Rahim, in his enthusiasm, declared the best support for her aging back. It smelled of rubber even through the sheets she'd brought from her daughter's house. Fatimah had agreed with her brother and added that a bed in this style was less likely to attract bugs. More than that, she'd bought the matching orthopaedic pillow, which for all of its quilted padding was as much foam as Rahim's bed.

Grandmother Jah rolled onto her back to better align her neck with the curve of the pillow. She tried sliding forward so that she was just at the edge, but still found that the pillow was too high.

The ceiling fan lumbered overhead. Though she'd personally never heard of a fan falling out of its socket, it sounded as though the motor was straining against the ceiling, and the fan blades whipped like a top on the verge of collapse. Their small breezes lapped at her cheeks and tossed fine hairs over her forehead, which she wiped aside.

She closed her eyes. There were no road sounds or cicada songs to accompany the air whisking around the room. Their land was one of the oldest plots in the village and the farthest from everywhere else. It was too dry a season for frogs, and the grass around the place too freshly cleared for crickets.

Bringing her hand to her side, she curled her fingers against the sheets. Her hand brushed a draft, cold, and in spite of itself, material. She bolted upright, pulling away the blanket from her legs. Instinctively, she kicked out at the space beside her. Her leg hit the same concentration of draft and cold her hand had met, registering it as a bulk that rolled away upon contact with her foot.

"Filthy old man!" she shouted. "Shameless!" Staring firmly into the darkness beside her bed, she lifted her hand and pointed. "How dare you come back here?"

The darkness was as impenetrable as the view had been behind her closed eyelids. Knowing but not seeing what lay there added to her anger, and her anger added to her voice. "This is my house. This is my children's inheritance. This has nothing to do with you."

The ceiling fan continued to spin overhead, though the air

it stirred had grown damper, with a brackish, almost muddy aftertaste. A choking feeling began to rise in her throat, as though the air conspired to thicken there. "Go back to your whore," she rasped, clutching the blanket to her chest. "Leave me alone."

The rattle of the fan's motor began to slow.

Grandmother Jah made an effort to breathe through her nose, which helped minimise the taste of soil, but brought her the full smell of dirt. Swinging her legs over the edge of the bed, she fished for the floor. The vinyl was cool to the touch, as if she'd plunged her feet into water.

She hobbled to the window, the glass panes shut against the night, where the lack of moonlight seemed to make the room colder. She ran her finger along the edge of the panes, counting upwards to the fourth pane, and slid her finger left till she hit the lever that opened the window. As she moved to grab the lever, she felt the chill rise up against her ankles. Four cold spots pressed into the left side of her foot and one cold spot pressed into the right.

A hand stroked her arm, from her shoulder to her inner elbow.

Grandmother Jah screamed as she slapped the head of the old man she knew, but could not see, was in the shadows. "Come near me again, will you? Just try to come near me again!"

She knew he raised his arms to shield himself from her blows. "It's not enough you married that whore."

Thud after thud she rained on him. "Your son loves another man, but he still has more dignity than you."

She knew he could hear her shriek. "If my descendants are never Malays, they would still have more dignity than you.

"Your daughter refuses to even come here. That's how

ashamed she feels." His ears, his wrists, his neck—she knew what her hands hit when they reached out. "You brought this on yourself."

She got a handle on his nose and pulled until he drew back. "Your legacy is nothing. I'll see to it. I'll make it so."

The hand on her foot let go.

Grandmother Jah reached for the window's lever and pulled. The zest of wild weeds and night flowers overpowered the scent of earth. Overhead, the fan began to pick up speed. The geriatric motor went back to making its mournful noise, and Grandmother Jah slumped against the window frame, resting her elbows on the recess there. She was sure, even if she kept her window open every night from now on, there wouldn't be a robber stupid enough to come in. Her pillow would soon absorb the pungency of her sweat and cease to smell of its factory. It was entirely possible that her back would improve with her son's new bed.

But she would miss the song of the cicadas until the grass grew taller, and strain for the frog calls until the monsoon came.

———

"Peace be upon you!"

The rattling of the grille was audible from the kitchen, where Grandmother Jah drank her coffee black and thin, with a hint of sugar. She adjusted her sarong beneath her faded batik nightshirt, both barely wrinkled by the night before. She'd returned to her bed but not retired, preferring to sit and wait for the birds at dawn.

"Is anyone home?"

She sipped from the rim of her cup, so her upper lip made waves in the drink. Then she put the cup down, perfectly aligning it with the centre of her saucer, and replied, "*And upon you be the peace.*"

Rising from her seat, she made the long trek to the front door, the dull ache in her legs today a little more bearable than usual. As she rounded the corner out of the kitchen and passed the telephone alcove, a large white shape fluttered down over her head. Grandmother Jah clawed at her face until it slid free and beheld the headscarf in her hands, long enough to wrap her from the top of her fringe to her waist. She looked up at the rafters, festooned with spider webs, and looked down once more. She'd never owned a headscarf this long, nor had she worn anything in the same style outside of her praying clothes.

She threw it on the stool beside the phone with a grunt.

Three men waited beyond the grille that protected her front door. Their lace skullcaps glared white on their dark heads, while they draped their shawls around their shoulders like women. All three bowed their heads at her presence.

"Can I help you?" she asked.

The eldest of them was as old as Rahim. When he spoke, he seemed to be keeping his gaze as stiffly on her face as he could manage, which was to say he quickly began to show his discomfort. "We came from the village. Uncle Ghani was an active member of our mosque."

Grandmother Jah unlocked the grille, pulled it a few inches out of its lock, and kept her hand on the handle.

"We came to welcome you." The eldest one spoke again. "When we heard you were moving in, we thought to see if we could help."

Grandmother Jah put her free hand on her waist. The

pressure on her nightshirt tugged her collar slightly open. "I've always lived here."

The men peered among themselves.

She flicked away an edge of her sarong with her foot. "This is my house," she explained. "I've only just moved *back* in."

"It's unfortunate about what happened to Uncle Ghani and Mrs Aisya." The youngest of the lot offered this morsel like a squirrel, twitching nervously from heel to heel. "Please accept our condolences for your loss."

"Well," began Grandmother Jah, and noticed the one member of the group who had not yet spoken was staring pensively at the curve of her breast, which hinted of itself at the corner of her collar. She pulled the offending side of her collar back into place, all the while looking directly at the quiet man, who veritably hopped in horror. "Well," she continued, "I thank you for your thoughts."

"Uncle Ghani was a good man. He's truly helped support the flock over the years," added the youngest.

"I'm sure the mosque meant the world to him," Grandmother Jah replied briskly. The quiet one seemed to shrink behind his peers the longer she stared back.

"Mrs. Aisya was a very kind woman. She was an example to all the ladies at the mosque," said the eldest.

At this, she focused her gaze directly upon the speaker, gripping the grille till she felt her knuckles whiten. "Young man," she asked, "have you married?"

"It is the duty of all able Muslim men to marry," replied the eldest, his face registering the most earnest confusion.

"Marry women of your choice, two, or three, or four. But if you fear that you shall not be able to deal justly with them . . ." Grandmother Jah nodded his way.

". . . then only one, or a captive your right hand possesses," ended the eldest mosque lackey. He cocked his head and fingered his chin, briefly turning to his friends, who looked away. "Auntie, why have you quoted the Quran?"

She shut the grille with a respectable slam. "If you can ask that, then you know that the only just number is one."

He clamped his mouth with obvious distaste, but kept his silence.

"Thank you for your concern. Please send my thanks to the mosque as well."

As they turned to leave, she gestured to the quiet man and said, "A pious man imagines clothes upon the unclothed. In any case, you're too young to attract the likes of me."

All three men burst into laughter. The quiet one was the first to utter his embarrassed, "*Peace be upon you,*" after which, the others followed suit.

Grandmother Jah smiled when she said, "*And upon you be the peace,*" but kept her eyes sternly on their backs until they left the compound. When no trace of them remained, she returned directly to the headscarf she'd left behind. Taking both ends of the wrap, she ripped it apart.

"Devil woman!" Shaking the torn cloth at the shadowed rafters above, she cried, "Don't tell me to wear this when you show your hole to any man who wants it."

She grabbed her breasts and pushed them upwards. "Each of these is old enough to be your grandmother." Shouting loud enough to scatter the spiders, she added, "You should be bowing at my feet."

Grandmother Jah collected the pieces of headscarf in a fist and walked back to the kitchen. Holding one edge over the stove, she flicked the knob of a burner and watched the spark it made flare to life. The soft material burned quickly, so quickly, she was forced to fling the cloth into the sink, the pungent smoke bringing her to tears.

"Grandmother Jah!"

She heard the grille open with a loud screech. Heavy footsteps ran down the hall. Loong appeared in the kitchen doorway, and before she could prevent him, he'd reached her side, running the tap at full blast.

"Are you all right?" he asked, as he swabbed the embers from the cloth. Long black scars ran down the pieces, broken by a mesh of char-eaten lace.

Grandmother Jah smiled. "I've been well."

"Why did you burn this?"

She wiped her eyes with a sleeve, and shook her head. "It's not mine."

Loong switched off the tap and gathered the cloth in his hands. Ashes drained through his fingers in flecks of ochre, like dried blood. With a twist, he squeezed the soot out of its threads.

"We should throw it away," she said.

He dumped it in the dustbin next to the sink. Later, when he'd boiled a fresh pot of water and topped up her coffee, he sat by her side till she ate the Chinese crullers he'd bought. Between mouthfuls of the chewy pastry, she explained the events of the night before, leading up to the headscarf.

Loong shook his head throughout, offering sympathetic exclamations. When she was finished, he said, "Spirits are bad, regardless of who they were."

"I don't want her spirit at all." Grandmother Jah set down her cup with a sharp clink and picked up another cruller.

"They must be reminded they're dead."

"I think she knows well enough she's dead," she replied, biting off a piece of pastry.

Loong curled his right hand around the bottom of his cup as he leaned back in his chair, the fingers of his left hand around the teacup's handle. "I know a nun. They say she sees spirits. Some friends have asked her before to bless their houses."

"Is she good?"

"I'm told her blessings work." He swung himself upright, eliciting a creak from his chair. "Grandfather Ghani and Mrs. Aisya must be put to rest."

"How soon can you get her?"

"I can ask."

―――

"Thank you for visiting me." Grandmother Jah ushered the nun through the gate, away from the sounds of the street outside. "I hope I haven't been too much trouble?" she added, as they passed beneath the arm of a bougainvillea's shadow.

Master Zhen was a tall, skeletal woman, with a square face and a knobbly chin. She nodded her acquiescence with a smile, and denied the hassle with a soothing, "No, no. No trouble at all."

It was a balmy day, untouched by breezes or dark clouds. The tree stumps had begun to darken amongst the moss, taking on the appearance of stone. Weeds pushed their shoots from the patches of earth between the roots, their foliage basking in the sun. As the nun crossed the garden, her grey robes matched the colour of the pavestones. Where the dew had not yet dried on the concrete, it mottled her path like shadow. Her eyes were clear behind her glasses, which she wore perched at the end of her nose. She'd attached the handles to eyeglass straps that she draped, as her only ornament, around her neck. They bounced lightly over her cotton wrap.

Loong followed behind both women, attentive to every word. He was there to translate in the event their English failed them and facilitate conversations the other way around. Now he hung back, a kind of bolster for Grandmother Jah's resolve.

The house stood squat against the morning light, the front grille thrown open to welcome its guests into the den, where tea cooled beneath the softly whirring ceiling fan and sofa cushions strained against their green covers.

They entered the house single file, with Grandmother Jah at the front and Master Zhen directly behind her. Grandmother Jah lifted her sarong to cross the threshold. A tiny cockroach raced across the plywood board as she did so, disappearing down a seam in the floor. At the corner where the door met the wall, she spotted beads of house lizard droppings.

Grandmother Jah stepped firmly into her home. With an outstretched arm, she said, "Please come in."

Master Zhen nodded, running her gaze around the room without a word.

Loong, who had waited for both women to enter before him, looked first at Grandmother Jah, before looking earnestly at the nun.

Master Zhen's head of black roots, trimmed like grass, glistened with damp. The shine on her face merged into a droplet, which she rubbed off her chin. Her eyes seemed to be focused on the hallway that led past the kitchen into the master bedroom. She took a step forward and angled her head, ever so slightly, before turning to smile at Grandmother Jah. "Loong told me there were two spirits here. One woman. One man."

Grandmother Jah caught herself in mid-frown, forcing it into a smile. "The woman is the troublesome one."

Master Zhen looked vaguely confused. "When all the spirits and people are not in balance, there can be no harmony."

"Yes, but I've only seen the woman lately," pressed Grandmother Jah. "She causes more problems for me, so I need her gone."

The tiles were sticky where her feet sweated upon them. The air clung to her in strings that grazed her neck and seeped down her collar. Grandmother Jah dabbed her sleeve against her throat to catch the moisture there, choking at the touch. Gesturing at the telephone alcove, she said, "I met her ghost over there." She added, hopefully, "A scarf fell from the ceiling."

The nun ambled towards the alcove, tilting her head upwards to peer at the rafters. Her pose reminded Grandmother Jah of a stork, tall and thin in the middle of a rice paddy.

Light from the front door stopped short of the beam that demarcated the space, silhouetting the furniture in shadow. The rectangular plastic telephone was an outline atop its stand, looming over the stool that waited beside it. Behind them, the wall seemed farther away than Grandmother Jah remembered. It seemed to suddenly curve ever so slightly around the stool and the stand, and just as suddenly, as if it realized she was watching, it sat perfectly still again, returning to being a straight board from end to end.

Master Zhen concentrated on the ceiling of the alcove with her back towards them. Finally, she turned around and shook her head.

Grandmother Jah restrained a huff.

Next to the nun's feet, she could make out traces of white soles with coffee-coloured heels. When the nun stepped forward, they followed her, left foot forward to her left foot forward.

Grandmother Jah crossed the floor in three strides, ready to step between them.

Master Zhen lifted a hand, signalling for her to be still. She stared quietly to their right. Pointing to the door only a few inches away from the television, she asked, "What's in there?"

Grandmother Jah glanced at the woman's feet. Her chauffeur had left.

"I think that used to be Rahim's room," offered Loong. "Her son," he added.

"That's right." Grandmother Jah strode to the door in question, and with her hand on the knob, she asked, "What can you see?"

"A child used to live here." Master Zhen walked to Grandmother Jah and placed her hand over hers, "But this isn't your child," she said. "His mother is crying."

Grandmother Jah stepped away, as the nun opened the door.

The room stretched from the door to the length of the futon beyond it and the window at the other end of the mattress. The glass was dark, smeared with fingerprints of light.

Dust veiled everything, from the shelves on the wall to the model cars that sat on them, arranged to face the door. Dust powdered the floor, where shoe prints criss-crossed the tiles in patches of pale green against brown.

She followed them as they skirted the mattress, to the edge of the mosquito netting that covered her son's old bed. Age stained the netting yellow and grime formed patches of grey. She carried her gaze up along the canopy to the crown from which it hung, and let it fall back upon the mattress where a pillow lay, round and wrinkled like a grub.

As she drew her gaze back, her eyes caught a trick of the light—a mark on the cotton that seemed faintly darker than the dirt. The mark sat high upon the mattress, curved like a sickle as it reached the bottom. It could've been, if Grandmother Jah allowed her imagination to run, the outline of a woman in prayer. It had to be a woman, she surmised, because the outline of a cloak wrapped around her could not be attributed to a man.

Beside her, Master Zhen lurched forward.

Grandmother Jah watched as her shoulders relaxed and her head slumped, though her eyes remained open. Her glasses, slipping ever more precipitously forward, finally fell off her face. The sweat had dried off her neck.

Master Zhen was shivering.

In perfect Malay, a voice too young and too girlish for the older, serious nun, she said, "*Peace be upon you.*"

Behind her, Grandmother Jah heard Loong thud against the door frame on his way out. To Master Zhen's face she said, "Get out. You don't belong here."

The nun shook along her entire spine, like an epileptic would. She looked back at Grandmother Jah in the eye, her face contorted into a frightened, startled mask. Without blinking, she asked, "*Won't you greet me, Sister?*"

Grandmother Jah glared.

In the moment that passed between them, she refused to let her gaze wander from the person in the nun's eyes, into the soul of the woman her husband had chosen.

The ghost wavered, breaking the line of sight by glancing here and there.

Master Zhen rasped, rattling the air out of her lungs. Though she stood completely still, it seemed that her voice paced the room, anxious gasps between desperate squeaks. "*I'm waiting for my son,*" she murmured. "*Have you seen my son?*"

"Don't change the subject, woman. You don't belong here."

The wheezing intensified, as the ghost's voice grew to a noise. "*My son was with me. Have you seen my son?*"

"Your son," Grandmother Jah began, noting the wet smear of saliva on the nun's lips, "Your son is dead."

"*Then—Why isn't he with me?*"

"Go find him in Heaven, if you know how." She spat the words at the spirit, watching as the death mask twisted further and the nun contorted into a scream of pain.

For a moment, Grandmother Jah wondered if she might collapse, and reached for her arms.

Master Zhen began to untangle from the ghost, the blood slowly returning to her face.

"Get out." Grandmother Jah repeated, firmly. "There is nothing for you here."

A tremor stretched across the other woman's arms as she folded over, looking as though she were about to retch. "*I bear witness that there is no God except Allah.*"

The nun's breathing dipped to a pause. Her shoulders tensed, and straightened. "*I bear witness that Muhammad is the messenger of Allah.*"

"It's too late to recite!" yelled Grandmother Jah. "You've already destroyed everything you could."

"*Sister!*" Master Zhen gasped. With Grandmother Jah's attention fully upon her, the ghost seemed on the brink of despair. Then, almost ashamed, she asked, "*Won't you even greet me, Sister?*"

Grandmother Jah turned away. Without remorse, she added, "And upon you be the peace."

Master Zhen nodded, her whole body falling limp. When the nun next lifted her head, she tucked her glasses back up against her face. Bringing her hands together neatly, she began to chant.

Grandmother Jah allowed herself to wait within her calm, letting her mind empty, even if it was for a short while.

When Master Zhen was done, she strode to the mattress and threw aside the canopy. In the middle of the bed, the pillow lay plumped on its side. Dust rose like a fog around the nun's robes.

Both Grandmother Jah and Loong coughed.

The nun knelt beside the pillow, stroking its head as one would a child. She briefly looked over her shoulder and said, "Women, when they give birth, need a strong will. That's why she stayed for so long. But," her hand fell, coming to rest on her knee, "No mother wants to see her child die."

Grandmother Jah leaned her elbow against the door frame, as Loong rubbed her back. "I'm not sure she stayed for her son."

The nun smiled. "Anywhere in the world, a mother's love is the strongest love of all. In Buddhism, we say that love between a man and a woman is the selfish love."

And in our religion, Grandmother Jah thought, *a stillborn child is its mother's shield from the fires of Hell*. Aloud, though, she said, "Can you make her go away?"

"*Amitabha*." Master Zhen pressed her palms together and bowed in turn. "I will pray that she does not return. She will find peace."

"Thank you," said Grandmother Jah softly, as the nun began another chant, this time lasting far longer as it curved and meandered through the air like a babbling brook. It was tranquil and perhaps, thought Grandmother Jah, its soothing effect was designed for both the dead and the living.

When she was done, Loong thanked the nun in Mandarin.

Grandmother Jah led Master Zhen by the arm towards the doorway. "Would you like some tea?" she asked. "You still look a little pale."

"Only if it will not trouble you."

"No. No trouble at all," Grandmother Jah responded, still smiling. Glancing at Loong, she added, "Loong, why don't you boil some water for us?"

He stepped back to let them through, replying with, "Yes, Grandmother. Right away," and left for the kitchen. On his way over, he peered quickly at the rafters of the telephone alcove, which made both women laugh.

Grandmother Jah noted that her husband's feet did not follow him.

————

The bomoh prepared strips of paper with a felt tip pen, breathing the name of Allah into vapours of frankincense. His calligraphy was brisk, tipped in hard angles. He worked with a black pen and a gold pen, dotting his accents with metallic ink. The candlelight shivered across his page. It felt as though it burned his words on wherever it flickered, making certain that even in the afterlife, his prayers could be heard.

Grandmother Jah sat before him, her legs folded to her side.

Her granddaughter set her hand on the mat beside her. The skin of her forearm was dark, the henna that coloured it almost charcoal in its vibrancy. A triplet of mangoes, ascending in size, climbed a trellis of butterflies' tongues from her wrist to the centre of her palm. Chains of ivy crossed her head- and her heart-lines, tapering to a single loop of fern feathers. It spanned her index finger and stopped, right beneath the nail.

What a wonder this girl, who looked as she had in her youth, with bold black curls and a bright doll's eyes, only perhaps, more beautiful. Grandmother Jah reached out her palm to pat her head.

Khatijah knew an Indian friend who hennaed for pocket money. Girls of the current generation, it seemed, dyed their fingertips and patterned their palms without first waiting for their marriage bed.

From the same source, Khatijah had found the bomoh. According to his reputation, he'd charmed at least one famous actress, and manoeuvred the marriages of many more from afar. It was Khatijah who'd brought him here.

When you need an outsider gone, you use an outsider to chase them away, Grandmother Jah thought. *When you need to keep away the familiar, you speak to it in words it understands.*

The bomoh finished his writing and shuffled the strips into a straight pile. With a hand wrapped around each edge of the pile, he said to the women, "Now, we need to put these above your doors."

He rose from the mat and turned towards the front grille.

Khatijah went to the telephone alcove to retrieve the stool.

As her granddaughter carried it into place, Grandmother Jah handed the bomoh pieces of tape she'd cut earlier.

He curled ringlets of tape around the end of his finger and pasted them to the back of one of the charms, before ascending the stool to stick it above the door frame. This he repeated for the other side of the door. When he cupped his hands to the height of his shoulders, the two women did the same.

"In the name of Allah, protector of all things on this earth and in the sky, for He is All-Hearing and All-Knowing."

They walked through the house in silence, the bomoh at the front, followed by Grandmother Jah, with Khatijah to tag at her grandmother's side. Her granddaughter held her tongue. Whether it was because she had nothing to say, or because she was caught up in it all, Grandmother Jah couldn't fathom. But Khatijah had been aghast when Loong told her about the exorcism.

Grandmother Jah had listened from Rahim's bedroom as they argued in the garage, as quietly as they thought they could.

But Khatijah still verged on shouting when she told him, "This is their house. Leave them to it."

"Your grandmother needs her peace." He'd laid a hand on her arm, which she'd shaken off. "The dead shouldn't be with the living."

"That's not it," her granddaughter whispered. "If she wanted the house, she already has it. But doing this is just petty."

"You didn't stop her from moving in."

"How could we have stopped her from moving in?" Khatijah shuffled her feet, twisting the edge of her tunic between her palms. She turned towards the garden, and squinted at something in the distance, before quickly looking away. "Look," she added, "I know you'd like to believe Grandmother Aisya is at peace—if you say so. But this house isn't worth it."

"We can't just leave it this way either." Loong put his hand on her arm again. This time, she didn't move. "We'll put both of them to rest. Let Grandmother Jah enjoy her retirement. It's already started, anyway."

Khatijah had returned to gazing at the shorn orchard, and seemed to stare overly long at the swings, which stayed utterly still. She'd nodded, slightly, but Grandmother Jah noticed how she refused to look at the garden when she passed it ever since that day.

Rahim was even less enthusiastic when he called.

"*Peace be upon you*, Mum."

"*And upon you be the peace*."

Behind him, she could hear the sounds of the kitchen, a hive of people over the clatter of pots and chopping boards.

"Mum," he'd said, "you should move out. We can put you up in a nice apartment somewhere. Anywhere you like. If you want to be close to the village, we can do that."

"This house is mine."

"Mum, it's in a good location. We can get a good price for the land."

"This house is yours too. When I'm gone—"

"Except you're not. You're still here."

"When I'm gone," she continued, firmly, "this land will be split between the two of you and you can do whatever you want with it."

"Big Sister doesn't want it. You've heard her."

"She'll have something that old man left behind. It was the least he could do."

There was a tap as he moved away from the receiver, and mumbled commands to people outside the conversation. When he returned, his voice took on a staccato and a clip. "Don't trouble Big Sister too much. She's had enough. And don't trouble Kat or her boy either. I'll talk more when I get home."

"You have nothing else to say."

A brief quiet enveloped the other end of the line, followed by a sigh. "Love you, Mum."

"Love you too."

She'd waited for him to hang up first.

In the present time, the bomoh wheezed. His breath stank of incense.

Grandmother Jah could smell it coming off his nostrils and bouncing off his palms.

She watched the charm affixed to the kitchen door frame. The thick white paper was textured to resemble stone, a left-over covering sheet from one of Khatijah's school projects. The pens came from a set her granddaughter had used to label her textbooks. The bomoh's handwriting formed fronds and tapers, collected at the bottom like bushels of garlic. She could barely read the ornamentation, but recognized the name of Allah well enough.

They moved to the master bedroom. Khatijah was responsible for the stool, and set it in front of the door. As before, the bomoh climbed it to stick a strip of paper on each side of the door frame. When he climbed down, they kept moving.

Grandmother Jah glanced back as they left. Through her bedroom door, she could see the window, shining on the floor with clear afternoon light.

They passed the telephone alcove. It was an empty dark corner, a sanctuary of dust. The phone sat on its bracket, polished matte by years of sweaty hands.

Soon, they passed the children's old bedroom. She'd thrown the door open in the morning, to help the air flow through the house. Shielded by the garage roof on the window side, it was always more shaded than the other rooms. The chill that wafted through was colder than anything formed by the natural shade. At the corner of her eye, where the door hid the end of the bare, sullen mattress, she caught a flicker, like the movement of an insect or a sunbeam.

"Pak," she said, stepping quickly to stay abreast with the bomoh, "maybe we should put the last one here."

"But this is for the gate," he replied. "It will keep all evils away from your house."

"All the evils," she said, "come from inside this house." As she pointed her thumb at that bedroom's door, she added, "This room is the worst."

The bomoh reached up to scratch the edge of his skullcap. "This is the last charm though. We won't have enough for both sides."

"Then, put it over this door." Grandmother Jah grabbed the stool from Khatijah and set it down in front of the children's bedroom.

For a moment, he stared at the open doorway, his eyebrows joined in a frown. In the end, he simply nodded and smiled. "Very well," he said. "We can put it here."

The bomoh adjusted the stool and hoisted himself up.

Khatijah handed him the last two segments of tape.

He rubbed the strip firmly into the wall as he applied it. Descending back to their side, he resumed his prayer.

"*Allah! There is no god but He—the Living, the Self-subsisting, Eternal.*" As he recited, he swayed from his waist to his forehead, drawing the words out and holding them, as the notes in a song.

Grandmother Jah closed her eyes as she cupped her hands to her chest. She tucked her elbows against her body, as she was taught from childhood, for devils liked to enter the gaps people left open when they prayed. Knowing what the bomoh quoted by heart, she mouthed the final lines with him:

"*. . . He feeleth no fatigue in guarding and preserving them, for He is the Most High, the Supreme in glory.*"

The door slammed shut.

They all looked up at the sound.

The stool scratched loudly across the tiles, stopped by the bomoh's feet.

He reached over to try the handle. It was stiff and locked. The bomoh tried pushing with both hands, even elbowing the top of the handle and leaning his weight in.

Behind him, the two women dropped their hands and never bothered to say "Amen."

Khatijah made as if to leave, perhaps to find a tool, but Grandmother Jah stopped her by grabbing her arm.

At the bomoh, Grandmother Jah simply placed her hand above the door handle and said, "Leave it. What is inside refuses to come out."

"But this is clearly wrong," he protested. "Something powerful is here."

Grandmother Jah shook her head, moving in to block the bomoh and her granddaughter from the door. "Because of what we did today, it can stay inside. That room can stay closed. One less thing for me to clean." Pulling an envelope from her pocket, she said, "Thank you for your kindness," while offering it to him with her hands in *salaam*. "Please take this small token as a gesture of thanks."

He accepted her gift with both hands. "I feel bad taking this. Your problem is still there."

"Don't be," she replied. Pursing her lips and pointedly facing the door, she added, "If it stays in there, this house is already a better place."

The bomoh glanced at the door one last time, a look of disquiet clear on his face. Finally, he said. "I will take my leave. But if anything happens, you should call me back."

"We will," said Grandmother Jah briskly. She gestured at Khatijah with a quick jerk of her head.

Khatijah responded with a mild look of alarm, but quickly smiled and said, "Pak, I'll send you back to the mosque. Is that all right?"

"That will be fine," he responded, warmly. "*Peace be upon you*," he added, to Grandmother Jah.

"*And upon you be the peace.*"

As they walked to the front porch, the glare of the afternoon made everything seem as though it were bathed in artificial lighting, the way daytime soaps and hospitals shared the same antiseptic sheen.

Khatijah bowed and kissed her grandmother's hands before stepping outside. Her grip was strong.

Grandmother Jah didn't lean in to touch her hair or wipe her brow, nor did she step beyond the front grille herself.

Her granddaughter helped the bomoh into the front seat of the car before getting in, never once facing the garden for more than a moment.

Grandmother Jah threw a glance at the swings beside the garage.

The figure of a woman, draped in white, sat on the edge of the seat. Her headscarf fell free about her face, hiding her as though she were behind a veil. She kept herself bowed over her lap, not caring to look up even as the car sped down the road.

Grandmother Jah returned inside. The grille shuddered as she pulled it closed, and the key rattled the iron to its bones.

She left the wooden doors open, to let out the incense that remained.

As she passed the locked bedroom, she heard the shuffle of feet, and watched as shadows paced beneath the door. They stopped when she touched the handle, staying in one spot, as if to face her on the other side. The metal was cold, as was the draft that brushed against her toes. Yet she was sure that nothing would open that door again. And God willing, no one would until she was dead.

With no one left in the house except them, Grandmother Jah allowed herself to smile.

———

"In the same way that a knife which has to cut all sorts of things may be of almost any shape; whilst a tool for some particular object had better be of some particular shape. Natural selection, it should never be forgotten, can act on each part of each being, solely through and for its advantage."

—*The Origin of Species,* Charles Darwin

Rahim

"Mum said to chop these down." Rahim looked up at his father's mango trees, each approaching twenty years old. The tallest trees soared above the house, with the smallest among them double his height and triple his girth. Fire ants blanketed the overripe fruit, so the mangoes appeared to bleed without spilling a drop. The fruit hung like burning lanterns well above the reach of the earthbound and were beyond the two men's reach in any case.

Bougainvillea grew over the garden paths like wild plumes of flame, partitioning the space between the trees with claustrophobic zeal. The vegetable patch by the chicken coop had long gone to seed, and where ants hadn't gorged on the produce, gashes showed the work of birds, perhaps mice. The house was two tiny bedrooms and a rust-spotted zinc roof. Its two bathrooms coughed up cockroaches from every grate. The house had stayed closed since the funeral, and neither Rahim nor Habib thought it best to air it out this late in the evening.

The idea was that they would handle the house in segments, clearing out a room at a time until all the main furniture was cleaned and the smaller pieces sorted. The garden though, his father's very pride, would have to go.

Habib served tea as Rahim perused the trees before settling down on the swings with a cup himself. His small frame made him appear like a doll with meatpacker's arms.

Rahim breathed in the scent of roses in his tea, wincing as the full perfume hit his nostrils.

Habib said, "I had to make do with whatever was in the house. Sorry if it smells like an old woman."

Rahim chuckled. "No, it's appropriate. Mother liked this flavour, and we are supposed to be the guests here, I think."

His friend shuddered as he looked over his shoulder. "Do you think we'll have ghosts?"

Rahim smiled as he shook his head. "If we do, we'll have to trust my dad not to lynch us in our sleep."

Habib wrinkled his forehead as Rahim said this. His usually bright eyes had seemed duller the moment they'd crossed the threshold of the house, and Rahim knew that Habib would worry himself into a fit if he could.

Rahim set himself down on the swing beside Habib, so the warmth of his shoulder would offer a small comfort to the other man. Habib's hand felt cold to the touch. Rahim regretted grasping it the moment he tried. "I'm sorry I had to bring you along for this. But you knew I couldn't do this alone."

Habib gave him a watery smile.

The effort forced Rahim to look away. "It's not like we're still children. If Mother and Dad do show up, we're the ones with the right to be here."

"But only for as long as it takes."

"Yes. We'll stay only for as long as it takes." Rahim articulated this slowly, taking care to aim the words directly at the house.

It was something his mother once told him: always tell the spirits how long you meant to impose. Otherwise, they might follow you home. It was a silly superstition. But these things had an order you respected out of habit.

"I don't get it. Why does your mum want this house back? I thought she hated your father at the end."

"She did. But she hated that other wife even more," Rahim replied, absently rocking himself on his heels. The chains creaked as the seat began to sway. "Anyway, the house has no value left since he died in it. It's better than leaving it alone."

"And you'd be the son to get all responsible about it." Habib leaned back with a sigh.

"I'm the only son she has."

They paused to sip their tea and let the light between the trees dapple them like jewels.

Quite suddenly, Habib pointed upwards. "Look, what's that?"

Rahim angled his head until he saw the branch overlooking the swings. A tiny brown spot drifted lazily towards him, landing soundlessly on his lap. He picked it up with two fingers, feeling the soft down crush like fine velvet, and looked at Habib with gentle puzzlement. "I think it's a chicken feather."

Leaping to his feet, Habib exclaimed, "The chickens! Oh, god. We forgot all about them."

The two men dashed to the back of the garden. Rahim cringed the whole time. *I've totally fucked up. The chickens are probably dead.* These thoughts bounced in his head the whole way.

Yet the little fenced-in yard for the chickens was utterly quiet, the coop totally empty, its door ajar. The plywood walls were dark with dust, and eggshells stuck like concrete to the hardened chicken droppings rubbed into the earth. In the mid-year heat waves, the zinc roofing would've melted the fat off the chickens under their feathers. Rahim remembered how, whenever they failed to hose down the roof when he was a child, there would be a massive pot of curry to share with the neighbours the next day.

Rahim was sure they never gave away any birds and no one had asked after them. He breathed a sigh of relief. "They ran away," he said. "It's just as well. They would've died if they stayed behind."

Habib stayed at the gate of the chicken compound with the tips of his slippers just touching the threshold. Every time he caught a glimpse of the ground, he quickly refocused his eyes elsewhere.

Rahim shook his head. "It's only dirt. I mean, it's been sitting empty for a month. The smell isn't nearly as bad as it used to be."

"You know I'm vegetarian," Habib replied.

"Right, so you should be happy the chickens are free."

"That cage is literally a death trap."

Rahim snickered and resisted the urge to simply drag Habib close. "Where are we sleeping tonight?"

"At the hotel." Habib now stared at him as though he had gone utterly insane. "The bed here has already been taken."

"I wanted to show you my old room."

"You can show me your old room in broad daylight. I'm not going into that house at night."

"You're not remotely curious?"

"No." Habib shuffled off down the garden path. As he walked, he called over his shoulder. "We're going home. The mosquitoes are starting to come out."

Rahim ambled after Habib, who'd begun to slap at his arms with gusto. Before he left, he remembered to shut the compound gate as a matter of habit. Perhaps, even the chickens feared ghosts.

———

". . . be kind to parents. Whether one or both of them attain old age in thy life, say not to them a word of contempt, nor repel them, but address them in terms of honour."

—*Surah Al Isrā', Ayat 23*

———

The next day, the sun battered the windows they threw open with hard light, and the heat choked the tiny rooms so desperately in need of air. They carried out all the paper waste they could into the living room, where the ceiling fan offered the slightest respite. Khatijah came over at noon during the worst of the heat. Rahim set his niece immediately on the task of bagging and carrying out the sorted garbage.

As she made the first few trips up and down the garden path, she tugged at the edges of her cream headscarf whenever she had a hand free. She slipped a finger beneath the rim of the scarf where it hugged her neck and flapped the folds over her bosom as if the two triangles formed wings. Habib tugged at Rahim's sleeve while her back was turned and hissed, "Don't you think it's better if the bigger person did all the carrying?"

When they stopped for lunch, Khatijah rested on the swing while Habib shared his rice box with Rahim inside, on the creaky rattan sofa with the dusty foam cushions. The curried rice stained Habib's fingertips red.

He bade Rahim take Khatijah her food before it got cold. Khatijah was staring idly into space as he walked out the door. She had her grandmother's, his mum's, round face, but was all bones everywhere else. Her tiny shoulders were hunched forward as she swung herself by the balls of her feet. The garden was a mass of overrun greens behind her, coloured by the occasional morning glory beginning to wilt.

Beside her sat a similarly-built woman, crouched over a wrapped bundle in her arms.

"Kat?" Rahim called out as quietly as he could.

His niece looked up at him without a trace of surprise. "Yes, Uncle?"

"Here. Why don't you have some lunch inside, with Habib?" Rahim held out her rice box as he walked up, coming to a stop directly in front of her knees. "It's cooler to be inside."

Khatijah accepted the food gracefully. "Thank you, Uncle." And tilted her head when he kept staring.

"Don't worry about me. I just wanted to use the swings too." He did his best to sound light.

When she hesitated, he added, "Habib is scared of ghosts. We shouldn't leave him alone."

This made her laugh. "All right," she said. "I'll keep him company," and wandered back inside.

The moment she left, Rahim occupied her empty seat and lost his smile. The lady beside him sat very still, the bundle carefully lying in the crook of her arm. Aisya had been exactly Khatijah's age. She was lithe, and had been extremely fair in life. Her nose bridge was high, and her eyes perfectly almond-shaped. Her lace headscarf was her only decoration over her dress. The sleeves covered half her hands, and the skirt reached the dirt beneath them. In her arms, buried in folds of swaddling, lay an infant with his face scrunched up and a single eye wrinkled shut, the skin tinged pale blue. Mother and child seemed to glow in the shade of the mango trees.

In lieu of any movement on Rahim's part, Aisya began rocking herself on the balls of her feet, just like his niece. It was such a natural reaction to being on a swing, even the dead could not help themselves.

Rahim considered her presence for a moment. His father's second wife had never been fond of speaking without first being spoken to. "Peace be upon you," he began.

"And upon you be the peace."

"Mother," he started again.

"Isn't he beautiful?" Aisya held out her child towards him.

Rahim kept his palms firmly curved on his knees. "He is, Mother."

His youngest brother had fine grey hairs at the top of his forehead, which clung to his skin with a damp film, like birthing slime. They'd found his newborn corpse on the front porch, alone on the concrete floor.

Aisya smiled gently. Rahim figured it was that sort of smile that had intrigued his father but disgusted his mother. She put a finger to her lips, and whispered, "He's sleeping."

Rahim nodded.

"I don't know how, but God doesn't think we're very pure. Your father knows."

Loud giggles emerged from the open doorway of the house, Habib's and Khatijah's. Rahim lifted his head in that direction.

Aisya went on. "Don't anger your father."

When Rahim turned back to her, she was gone. But to the air where she had sat he said, "I'll try not to."

———

"I was the one who found Youngest Uncle. I helped Grandmother Aisya deliver him." Khatijah leaned over the gate of the chicken coop, fingering the splintered wood frame.

Habib leaned his plump self against the wall opposite the coop, keeping himself well away from where the chickens lived. "I heard. It must've been horrible."

"Not really." Khatijah pulled a leaf off a dying vine and began rolling it between two fingers, like a tiny cigarette. "I ran when Grandfather threw Youngest Uncle down. After that, by the time we came back—I wasn't alone when we found them."

Habib stepped forward to put his hand on her shoulder. "It still must have been hard."

Khatijah slowly shook her head from side to side, the way an animal swayed when it was unwell. Her headscarf was textured with geometric shapes whose facets glittered like sequins when she moved. "The men said I shouldn't have gone inside, but I did. The way he held her, they could've been asleep."

"Once again, it still must have been hard." Habib shut his eyes and looked away, before scratching the back of his neck absently. "Hey," he began. "You're starting uni soon, right?"

"Yes, my first semester is in July."

"Really? All the best with that."

A short distance away, Rahim sorted yellowed newspapers into piles. Random text in Arabic script flowed beneath his hands. Every so often, a word in Jawi would make sense to him. Most of the letters were things he'd forgotten a long time ago.

"I'm surprised they didn't eat Youngest Uncle while no one was looking."

Rahim looked up.

"Who?" asked Habib.

"The chickens," replied Khatijah. She had a familiar, impish smile, one Rahim knew from his mother to his sister and now her. "We've never seen them since."

"Oh, Kat," Habib said sagely, "Chickens don't eat people."

"Grandfather's chickens ate mice," offered Khatijah. "That day, they were flying above the house."

"Chickens don't fly," Habib continued, but went slightly pale as searched the sky. Muttering under his breath, he quickly wandered back inside.

Rahim crossed the path to his niece and gave her a friendly slap behind her head. "Chickens don't fly," he said firmly. "At least, not normally."

Khatijah looked straight back at him, her large eyes clear and bright. "It really happened."

"As your grandfather would've said, 'that was the chickens defending their territory.'"

———

"Nor ought we to think that the occasional destruc-tion of an animal of any particular colour would produce little effect: we should remember how

essential it is in a flock of white sheep to destroy every lamb with the faintest trace of black."
—*The Origin of Species,* Charles Darwin

———

Rahim accompanied Khatijah as far as the bus stop. She'd insisted on finding her own way home. Habib had curled himself on the cushions in the living room when Rahim returned. He breathed slowly, his dark curls tossed over his face like combed wool.

Habib in sleep was like a resting cat, leaning towards the pale sunlight that arced across the floor and swept the edge of the sofa. Rahim sat on the floor next to his head. The rattan frame prodded his rib as he moved closer to sleep, the smell of dust rising from the upholstery between them. Rahim dimly began to miss their hotel, its clean sheets and the closed space it provided. Catnapping beside Habib was such a rare pleasure since they returned to Malaysia. Even the hotel room had twin beds.

Seen through half-opened eyes, Habib's body seemed to cast more shadows than it normally should. Rahim became aware of these shadows, at first a single mass that was far too big for a man of Habib's size, slowly splitting into two distinct images. The one shape began to move away from the other, almost stepping out of Habib's outline, until it loomed over Habib's shadow, very distinctly a person all his own.

All his own, because by now Rahim was aware that it was a male shadow over Habib's sleeping one, a shape he knew from the bond of father and son. Rahim watched in numb horror as his father's ghost-shadow reached for his beloved's body, not capable of even the strength to make the other man wake. In his mind's eye, a mirror image played on the wall: Dad standing over the sleeping Habib in the flesh, Dad with his gardening shears in hand. Habib, his innocent mouth curled at the edges as he slept, did not feel or sense the ghost. Even the idea of vengeance was alien to him, a trait for which Rahim loved him best.

The blade of his father's shears opened over Habib's throat.

Rahim did not turn his head to face his father, yet he could well imagine the fury with which his father uttered the words to sanctify slaughter: "In the Name of Allah, the Beneficient, the Merciful."

Lunging forth to shield Habib's body with his own, Rahim held Habib until the last whisper of, "God is great." His father's presence wavered and flickered away, like a coiled wisp of smoke. The pain in Rahim's heart was great.

Sunlight permeated the dust, fierce and fine. It reminded him of sitting under mosquito netting as a child, unable to tell if the light meant the start of the day or its end.

Habib began to stir. Eyelashes thick between semi-open eyelids, he asked, "Are we going to see your room?"

"I'd thought you didn't want to," Rahim replied, stroking Habib's brow.

"Since we're here. It seemed to matter to you."

They walked side-by-side, elbows touching. Rahim refused to grasp the other's hand for fear his shaking fingers would betray him.

His old room was neat, if not clean, the shelves arranged with toys and not-quite-ragged books. Dust clung to the floor and their shoes like gum. His father would have rolled in his grave just for wearing shoes in the house. What did his mother want here? Even her memories had long been buried beneath others.

Habib walked into the room first, seeking the window, where wrought iron blossomed out of the box hanging outside, the ever-living profile of a garden that hadn't changed since Rahim was a child.

A gutted cockroach lay legs-up across the windowsill. Habib winced when he noticed, turning to face Rahim with a weak smile, and leaned forward as if he had something to say. But there was nothing to say. It was an empty, dusty room. So Habib leaned back, just a smidgen, and let his smile fade.

Pushed right against the upper corner of the room was a futon, which waited beneath a tent of mosquito netting, silent and empty but for the bulge of a pillow at its head. Rahim made as if to open the netting and froze, his fingers just scraping the rough edge of air holes that told him the air inside this tent, this slice of private air, was cold, as cold as his insides had been when his father's ghost laid the scissors on Habib's throat. As for the pillow, it bundled itself in a fat heap on his old futon, still and rounded at the edges, seeming to sleep on its side.

Habib opened his mouth. The words came out dry. "Did you want to take your pillow home?"

Rahim tried not to look aghast. "Cute," he said. "But that's not my pillow."

"You look so sad though. I can imagine you as a little boy, trying to sleep with your friend the pillow."

"No, that's not my pillow."

"Well, stop staring at it."

"This is getting stupid. You didn't want to look at my room."

"I want to go home."

"Well, then we'll go home."

Habib searched his face, looking pained, but forcibly unflustered. "I'll wait outside."

Rahim shrugged.

Habib walked out somewhat faster than Rahim liked. He'd wanted one of them to be brave, especially the unknowing one, because ignorance created the best form of bravery.

Taking a half-step back away from the futon, Rahim moved right to the edge of the mosquito netting, away from what lay sleeping underneath. He strode to the window, reaching between the bars to lock it down, even though the bars alone would've given a burglar far more trouble than it was worth.

He did this even though he was scared, even though he didn't want to be here any longer.

When he made his way out, he faced the shelves rather than the bed. As he passed the bedroom door, he reached for the knob behind him and shut it as he had the window—tightly—because there was nothing worse than memories running amok. A light whisper rose from behind it, like the murmur of a feminine voice over a child at bedtime. Rahim shut out the words, not wanting to know.

Habib waited in the garden, stomping away mosquitoes from his feet. He reached for Rahim's hand. Their fingers stayed locked until they reached the lane where the house met the main road. What would the neighbours say if they saw them? It was only in the safety of their hotel room that they dared hold hands again.

"Yes, Mum. We've cleared everything."

"Have you cleared all of that woman's things?"

"I think we got almost everything."

"Just leave it on the kerb. The rubbish collectors will get it."

"Do you want to leave something for the mosque?"

"What's there to leave? Leave it on the kerb. If anyone else wants it, they can take it. But I don't want any of her things in my house."

"All right, Mum."

"Are you coming for dinner?"

"Not tonight. I don't think so."

"Come tomorrow."

"Okay."

"Bring your friend."

"Okay."

"Take care."

"Take care too."

Rahim shut the flap of his cell phone and watched the contractors haul the last of the branches away. All across the garden, twenty tree stumps, each framed by red brick paving, lay freshly chopped and naked. The creeping morning glories were gone, exposing trails of fire ants over the moss-grown earth. A man kerchiefed like a bandit hacked at the bougainvilleas. Papery lanterns of magenta, white and purple fell, but light flooded the garden more brightly than before.

They never did figure out what to do with the chicken coop, and Habib never set foot near it again. Rahim could just make out the top of the zinc roofs above the gate, where vines still shaded the corrugated metal from the sun. Perhaps his mother would restore it or hack it down.

He pulled the receipt from his pocket and handed it to the man with bougainvillea petals on his pants legs, who gave him his change, and shouted for his boys. Habib emerged from the house and locked the front door behind him. They would leave with the workers, among the sounds of life.

His father's ghost watched from among his felled trees, a presence more than a man. He was just an outline of his form, sullen-faced, with his eyes hidden. Rahim looked towards him, waiting for recognition, and found none.

Habib walked on ahead, laughing at something a worker said.

To his father, Rahim bowed his head. "*And upon you be the peace.*"

Ghani I

"*Man We did create from a quintessence (of clay);
then We placed him as (a drop of) sperm in a place
of rest, firmly fixed; then We made the sperm into a
clot of congealed blood; then of that clot We made
a lump; then We made out of that lump bones and
clothed the bones with flesh; then We developed out
of it another creature. So blessed be Allah, the Best to
create!*

After that, at length, ye will die."

—*Surah Al Mu'minūn, Ayat 12-15*

GHANI FINGERED THE MOIST SOIL OF HIS NEWLY PLANTED SPINACH
bed. *The loose grains on his skin felt light, as if they were filled
with the breath of the universe itself. The gardener worshipped
the Garden in its likeness, though as any good gardener would,
Ghani knew there was no gain in imitating God. But as far as
imitating Eden went, he figured his own small plot was not bad.*

Mango trees towered over the roof. Beneath their shade, chickens flapped and clucked in their enclosure, golden chickens that laid eggs for breakfast and fed the guests curry during Aidilfitri. Bok choy and water convolvulus grew green and broad-shouldered for the taking. Bittergourds, eggplants and winter melons hung heavy on frames by the kitchen door. All over the garden, shadowed corners were set ablaze by bougainvilleas, each flower a little paper lantern the colour of a jewel.

Ghani's granddaughter read a book on the swings. Khatijah was a tiny, skinny girl of seventeen-years-old. Her dress covered her toes when she sat down, and the edge of her headscarf always caught in her fingers when she turned a page.

She came to their house on Saturdays, in the evenings after the Islamic Girl Guides meeting at school. She took the bus home after tea, or when her parents called on her cell phone, whichever came first. As she read, she rocked herself gently on her heels. The swings creaked comfortably in response.

"Don't you get dizzy reading like that?" Ghani leaned on his spade and watched as she looked up. Khatijah was round-cheeked and round-eyed, like a doll. It made her head seem too large for her bony frame, and even though she swathed herself in a headscarf all day, her skin was as dark as the loam in her grandfather's vegetable beds. When she smiled, her smile was exactly like the elder Khatijah—his first wife. When she frowned, the resemblance made Ghani look away.

Aisya came up the path bearing drinks. She had a similarly small build, but was lithe and extremely fair, with a high nose-bridge. Ghani looked upon his wife with the pride of both a new husband and a new father. Although exactly Khatijah's age, she was already a real woman, her belly round and swollen with life.

Khatijah helped herself to the cream biscuits she brought and took small sips of the cordial offered.

For Ghani, there was a cup of plain tea, strongly scented with rose petals.

"What are you reading?" asked Aisya as she sat on the swings.

"Biology. We have a quiz on Monday." Khatijah pointed to a fetus on her page. "See? That must be what Youngest Uncle looks like now."

Aisya rubbed her belly and chuckled. "I don't know. Maybe." She peered at the book for a moment, and fingered a different illustration close by. "That's a cute baby, though."

"That's a mouse," Khatijah said.

"Oh." Aisya held her hand over another page. "But they look so alike."

"They all do when they're small. See? That's really a bird." Khatijah chuckled. "Grandmother wasn't wrong. We all really look like animals when we're babies."

"Don't say things like that," Ghani hissed. "It's making light of God."

His granddaughter gave him a measured look, and turned away to stare into her glass. "Yes, Grandfather," she replied.

Thus mollified, he sipped his tea. The brand Aisya liked to buy was an amber-red brew, which turned the clear glass cup the colour of his granddaughter's cordial. It was richly sweet like its perfume.

Aisya shook her head, clutching a spot below her navel. "All this talking must be waking Salih."

Khatijah perked up, leaning over to pat her belly. "Has Youngest Uncle been behaving well?"

"He's been kicking around, but he's been a good boy," Aisya smiled. "Isn't that right, dear?"

"Yes, he has." Ghani leaned his spade against the wall, coming to stand beside his wife and feeling like a tall reed next to the two women. "Your Uncle will grow up to be a very naughty playmate for you."

"Oh, don't say things like that. What if he hears you?"

They laughed hard enough to match the crows retreating at last light. Khatijah kissed Aisya's hand and then her grandfather's, promising that she would visit again before she left.

———

"Dear, call for you."

"Peace be upon you."

"And upon you be the peace. Dad, how are you?"

"Rahim!" Ghani clutched the phone with a hand that still smelled of compost. He quickly switched it to his other hand, which smelled of grass. "How are you doing?"

"I'm doing well. Things have been tiring, but also very exciting. There's just so much running around trying to keep track. I really miss everyone there. But I've got good news." Rahim's excitement added to the crackle of the line. In the background, there was the light clatter of plates and barked orders. Rahim drew a quick breath. "My contract here will end at the end of this month. I've been looking at ways to get all my things back to Kuala Lumpur. God willing, I'll be home by April."

"That's wonderful. Have you told Big Sister or your mum yet? I'm so happy for you."

"Big Sister knows. She's already planning a feast for the reunion. I'm planning to call Mum tonight. How are Mother and Little Brother?"

"Mother is keeping well. The doctor says Little Brother is

healthy and will be arriving on schedule. He should be born when you're here to greet him."

"That's good. Please send my regards to Mother and Little Brother, too."

"I will."

"What else is new there?"

"Khatijah just heard that she was accepted into the International Islamic University. We're all very happy."

"Wow, that's great. Congratulate her for me."

"Yes. She wants to take up journalism. I think that's a bit dangerous for a girl, especially if she gets assignments to bad countries, but you know Khatijah. She's very stubborn. That's your mother in her."

"She's fully grown now, Dad. Khatijah is a smart girl. I'm sure she knows what she's doing. Anyway, these days everybody does things with computers, so it's not like you have to be in a dangerous place any more to be a journalist."

Ghani propped himself against the desk by his fingertips, rubbing at the stain his fingerprints left behind. *"I don't know. Maybe she'll change when she gets married."*

"Maybe." During the pause on the line, Ghani could make out more barked orders beyond Rahim's back. *"Dad, I have to run. They're getting chaotic over here, and I better dive in before someone else complains. I just wanted to say hi and tell you I'll be home soon."*

"Ah, very well –"

"Send my regards to Mother. I'll talk to you again soon."

"Of course. I –"

A telltale beep came before he could finish. Ghani breathed into the receiver and heard his own sigh return with the crackle. Children these days.

Kat

"I have hitherto sometimes spoken as if the variations—so common and multiform in organic beings under domestication, and in a lesser degree in those in a state of nature—had been due to chance. This, of course, is a wholly incorrect expression, but it serves to acknowledge plainly our ignorance of the cause of each particular variation."
— *The Origin of Species,* Charles Darwin

———

KHATIJAH LEANED ON THE GATE AS IT SHUT BEHIND HER. The bag she held crinkled lightly against her knees. Steam collected in droplets against the thin plastic film, wetting her knuckles. The scent of caramelized onion followed by the astringent note of turmeric would occasionally filter upwards, making her stomach growl. It was a long way to the curry house, but Grandmother Jah preferred her biryani without the sultanas.

All along the garden path, the stumps of Grandfather's orchard were overgrown with moss. Petals of bougainvillea clung to the thorns that piled against the corners of his land, all that was left of the bushes that once thrived there. Swept into drifts by the wind, dried leaves twisted like spent cocoons, huddled against the pavestones. The call of cicadas swarmed out of the tall grass, though nary a bug could be seen. Among the dead roots, lizards scurried between the shadows.

Khatijah chewed on a cardamom pod as she walked, running the bag over the weeds that bordered the trail to the kitchen door. The mild bitterness of the spice spread across her tongue, sweetening her breath. As she went past the garage, she glanced at the swings between what had been Grandfather's oldest mango trees. The decapitated stubs looked like grave markers—the taller stub marking the head, and the shorter one the feet. The ground smelled dampest there, beckoning her to sit in the musty earth.

Khatijah blew into the air and quickly inhaled. The trace of cardamom in her breath blocked the smell of mud and the lingering decay that followed.

The sounds of dusk whirled overhead, in a triangle of crows that burst into caws; in the low murmur of mosquitoes as they rose out of the undergrowth; and the soft choking of a woman's muffled cries.

The small figure of that woman, draped in white, sat on the swings. As she wept, she rocked herself by the balls of her feet. She clenched and unclenched her hands to the rhythm of her shaking head, alternating between pounding her knees with her fists and burying her forehead in her palms.

Her headscarf fell over her face, completely covering her cheeks. Beneath its folds, a slender crescent of skin teased the onlooker, the way the moon teases its beholder in an eclipse.

"*Peace be upon you*," greeted Khatijah.

The woman did not look up, nor did she cease crying.

"Grandmother Aisya," she called again, "I'm home."

Grandmother Aisya shook her head. The fine lace of her headscarf, looped with roses, shivered like a cascade of withered vines.

"I'll be heading inside now," Khatijah said. "I must take your leave."

For the longest time before she moved in with Grandmother Jah, Khatijah had tried her best not to acknowledge the ghosts. Common wisdom said that if you did not acknowledge a ghost, it would not acknowledge you. If a ghost bothered you, acknowledging it just gave it power. But whatever else anyone might think, it was rude to pass by an elder without acknowledging them. When she was certain that Grandmother Aisya truly had nothing to say, Khatijah gave her a nod and continued briskly to the kitchen door.

It took a shove and some wrestling with her key, but she was soon inside the house. She left the door open with the grille locked behind her for air, placing her bag on the dining table.

Shadows leaned in from the windows alongside. Like lengths of dark gauze, they wrapped themselves over the counter tops and streamed against the shelves. What little light there was glanced off murky jars, where faded shapes took the colour of the monochromatic dusk.

Crossing into the hallway, she heard only silence. She

followed the wall to Grandmother Jah's door and knocked but received no reply. Opening the door as quietly as she could, she watched her grandmother kneel on the floor in prayer.

Grandmother Jah was draped in white with only her face and her hands exposed. She turned to greet unseen worshippers on either side. Greeting your neighbours was a good habit, which prayer reinforced as ritual, even though her grandmother had not attended mosque services for years.

Khatijah waited for Grandmother Jah to remove her headscarf before she stepped forward, kneeling at her grandmother's knees. She took the hand she was offered between both her palms and kissed its knuckles. "*Peace be upon you,* Grandmother."

Her grandmother patted her gently on the shoulder, before stroking her head. "Well," she said, "Did she give you any trouble today?"

"No, Grandmother. She never gives me any trouble."

"Don't be so confident," her grandmother replied, pulling away. "One of these days, something will happen. Then it'll be too late."

Khatijah shrugged.

Grandmother Jah rose to her feet, carrying her prayer coverings with her. "What did you get for dinner?" she asked.

"Biryani." Khatijah rolled up the prayer mat while her grandmother put away her things. When this was done, she withdrew to the door. "I got oxtail soup too."

"That sounds delicious."

Khatijah nodded, turning back towards the hall. "It's dark in here. I'll turn on the lights."

The hallway was filled with the still, pleasant air of the dry season, a small comfort to make up for the sun-baked days.

Before heading to the kitchen, she felt for the lights and turned them on. She found the mosquito repellent sticking to an outlet beside the TV and switched that on too. Glancing at the ceiling, she saw the faint outline of insects rising towards the beams, camouflaging themselves against the wood. With the repellent in place, they would not leave the rafters until dawn.

By the time she entered the kitchen, Grandmother Jah had already begun pouring out the soup.

Khatijah grabbed the box of biryani and a plate.

"Aren't you eating?" her grandmother asked.

"I will. I'm waiting to take anything you don't want."

"Then just give me half the rice."

Grandmother Jah shook the soup bag. Flecks of grey ox blood and chopped coriander slid into bowls of steaming broth. "I'll be eating with my hands," she added, carrying the bowls to the dining table.

Khatijah opened the box with a snap. The full smell of cumin and pepper drifted upwards into her face, along with all the other treasures buried in the rice. She spooned half of it onto the plate, making sure most of the fried shallots went onto her grandmother's share. Pausing briefly to survey her work, she spooned another quarter of the rice out for herself.

"That's too little," her grandmother said, peering over her shoulder. "Give yourself more."

Khatijah shook her head, gripping the spoon like a blunt knife. "I'm not really hungry."

Grandmother Jah bustled around her, reaching into a drawer for another spoon. "If you don't eat, your parents will think I don't feed you."

"My parents know I'm picky."

She rapped her granddaughter's knuckles with the back

of her spoon. "I'll not have it said that I look fatter than my grandchildren," she muttered.

Khatijah smiled. But she took just another spoonful out of the box.

When she joined her grandmother at the table, the older woman was already slurping at her soup. She sat down beside her in silence.

The oxtail soup was thick and greasy. Chunks of bone sat at the bottom of her bowl, and Khatijah scooped these out eagerly, sucking on the meat that still clung to them until the tendons melted away. Before she knew it, a pile of dried bones sat beside her bowl and only the murky broth remained.

"I thought you weren't hungry," her grandmother remarked.

"It's good soup," Khatijah answered, putting the bowl to her lips.

"Is that what it is?" Grandmother Jah chuckled.

Flustered, Khatijah tipped the bowl back until it covered her face. "I should finish it while it's hot."

Overhead, flying ants gathered around the ceiling light. Their flitting bodies made the bluish-white light seem to tremble. Behind her grandmother, she could see the garden, as much as the light from the kitchen illuminated through the grille. The ridges of tree stumps amassed in the distance. The swings could barely be seen. Only the curve of its outer frame showed, a colourless outline that seemed to blur into the undergrowth around it.

There, a flicker of white seemed to glow, like the very faintest candle flame through frosted glass. As she stared, the flickering seemed to stop, even solidify into an opaque mass. Khatijah quickly looked back at her food, but she knew it had caught her looking.

Ignore me, she pleaded, silently. *Go away*.

At first, it seemed like a stray piece of cloth that had blown off someone's clothesline. It folded in upon itself as it moved, looking bigger and smaller by turns.

Far too soon, it was halfway up the path—the short, slender figure of a woman draped from her forehead to her ankles in prayer clothes.

Within a heartbeat, it was at the grille, a woman dressed as much for mourning as she was for worship. Like all devout women, Grandmother Aisya wore her prayer shroud to her grave.

The light pouring out of the kitchen made her skin appear even more ghostly, like the complexion of a newsreader on a harshly lit TV set. And rather than make her disappear into the background, death had made Grandmother Aisya even more well-defined.

Khatijah could see the aquiline nose that was alien to her line of the family and the dark, despairing look in her eyes. When her lips peeled apart and didn't stop, widening into a gaping scream, Khatijah looked away.

Grandmother Jah bolted to her feet. Without so much as a glance, she slammed the kitchen door shut, and twisted the key like an errant grandchild's ear.

"Foul woman." She turned to her granddaughter, her voice grim. "One of these days, something bad will happen. Preferably to her."

"Hi, Mum. How are things?"

The weekly call was an arrangement they had. It prevented

her mother from calling whenever she pleased. As it was, Khatijah already found this a chore, but dealing with a voice on whom she could hang up was easier than dealing with a face.

Her mother's chair squeaked as she leaned back. "Did something happen?"

"No," Khatijah added quickly. "Grandmother's okay."

"That's good to know."

She heard the whirr of an air conditioner in the background, followed by the clacking of keys. There was the rasp of static over the line, as though her mother was speaking to her with the mouthpiece too far away from her lips.

When her mother paused, she could almost hear her think. "Are you okay?"

"I'm fine," she replied. "How are you?"

"I'm good."

Khatijah slipped her fingers around the telephone cord and began winding it around her hand. She waited for her mother to continue, as she often did.

"My boss asked me to look after the Kajang project last week. This week there were problems in Melaka, so I had to drive there. In two months, they'll begin work in Subang—"

"That sounds busy—"

"I'm tired, Kat."

Khatijah murmured in sympathy, tilting her head back to look at the rafters. She stared at the dark crevices between the wooden beams until the dust motes there appeared to quiver, listening to her mother breathe. "I'm sure you must be," she finally replied.

"I don't get home until late in the night. Even your father says I've lost weight." On cue, her mother began to sound even more ragged, as though the weight of the world rested on her shoulders. "I think I've gotten paler."

Khatijah leaned against the wall next to the phone, which seemed grey only because the alcove she sat in was dark. In a different light, it would be white, with tiny bubbles to pock-mark its surface. "You've always wanted to be fairer," she said, the only thing that came to mind.

"If I stand next to your father, even he might look darker than me."

"He might," Khatijah replied. The women of their family took after Grandmother Jah, both her mother and herself. They had the skin Malays called, 'sweet and black', like the coffee Grandmother Jah had with her toast every morning. Her father was pale, the parchment yellow that passed for fair along the Equator, but her grandmother's genes proved dominant.

Her mother fidgeted in her seat again, making the PVC beneath her creak. "Is everything really okay there?"

"We're fine. Grandmother's always tired, but I'm trying to stop her from doing the housework."

"That's good. Your grandmother's old. She shouldn't strain herself."

Khatijah smiled. "How's Dad?"

"Your father is getting fatter. He blames it on me, like I've infected him with it. He's the one who's eating too much."

"Dad deserves to enjoy himself."

"Maybe." Her mother laughed. "Your father has worked hard all his life. When I see him happy, I'm happy too." She drew another breath, which made the static on the line continue to wheeze.

Khatijah exhaled, deliberately making it sound like a sigh.

Her mother took the cue. "All right, I need to get back to work. I still have a lot to do."

"Send my regards to Dad."

"I will."

"Take care," Khatijah said.

"Take care," her only reply.

Khatijah put the phone down before her mother did. It was force of habit, to avoid hearing dead air.

The evening had still felt young when she began the call. Now, even though sunlight burned through the front grille, the stillness just before sunset prayers seemed oppressive. Khatijah walked over to the TV, tuning it to one of the new Chinese channels. She waited for the call to Maghrib prayers. Unlike the older networks, they showed footage from Mecca, where the muezzin wailed at length and with feeling, his voice rising over worshippers circling the Sacred Mosque.

On the screen, the Kaabah was the calm in a storm, a simple velvet cube at the focus of a brilliantly lit mosque. The scene, and the feelings it represented, was sweeping, not meditative. It helped force away any other thoughts she could have had.

"Is it Maghrib already?" Grandmother Jah rounded the corner from the kitchen, a cup of tea in her hand.

Khatijah looked up and smiled. "Yes. I got caught up talking to Mum. She sends her regards."

"Why is she sending her regards when she lives in the same city? It's not that far for her to drive." Grandmother Jah sipped her tea. "Your mother takes her work far too seriously."

"She works hard." Khatijah shrugged. "Would you like to eat right after praying?"

"I would," her grandmother began, and squinted at her comically. "You're not skipping prayers that easily."

"What made you think I was doing that?" Khatijah shook her head, her smile widening into a grin. "Even if I pray, we have to eat dinner."

"Maybe. But you know, your parents weren't very good about some basic things. If I don't bother to teach them to you, what will I say when I finally face God?"

Grandmother Jah shuffled back into the kitchen before she could reply.

Prayers, both as a ritual and a habit, were a staple of her grandmother's life. She wondered sometimes if, like her grandfather had, Grandmother Jah kept time by them.

Quietly, gathering her dignity around her like a cloak, she stood up. Between Maghrib prostrations and dinner, Khatijah preferred to settle dinner first. After all, someone had to be responsible.

———

Khatijah boiled porridge under rows of her grandmother's mismatched crockery. Jars of pickles stood on the lowest shelves, at the level of her neck. Over the years, the jars had shrunk in tandem with her grandmother, from the veritable urns Khatijah remembered looking up to as a child, to the used coffee jars of today, pieces of labelling still clinging to their corners.

She went for the smallest of these she could see, agitating the rickety shelf as she did so. The water behind the glass swirled up a plume of red that spread in a slow, expanding fog. Chilli flakes revolved like bits of raw meat around a white core. The swaying liquid made the pickle appear to pulse, like a heart, that having been bled dry, was only now beginning to drown.

Khatijah drained the cold brine into the sink, which washed down the drain the colour of faded crimson, and laid the vegetables on her chopping board. The smell of fermenting cabbage juice was strong, the very tart scent of death held at bay. She sliced the leaves thin, ready to garnish a saucer covered in a craquelure of fine stress lines, chipped even before it had reached her grandmother's collection.

Lowering the flame, she opened the lid of the stock pot. Inside, slivers of chicken breast floated on the skin of the porridge, cooked to a tender bite. Steam dampened her face, and when she moved just out of its range, she was cooled by the sweat rising out of her pores.

She grabbed the salt grinder, which, in her hands, felt heavy and immutable. It was an old-fashioned wooden kind, but nonetheless an improvement over using a mortar and pestle. The grinder's lacquered surface was richly grained, patterned with wide swirls of orange and cream. Its revolving top had gotten so loose after years of use, she had to struggle to get traction going for the metal teeth below.

She huffed as she worked, trying to ignore the warmth that continued to buffet her face. The pot wafted heat in a constant plume, while the kitchen's ventilation—what little of it there was—teased her with the barest hint of a breeze. Specks of salt freed themselves with a slight shake, only to melt the moment they hit the steam. The knob grew damp from her efforts, and she tightened her grip in response. After a good ten twists or so, she stopped to taste her work.

The porridge was still on the bland side, but the pickles would make up for it.

A sudden movement caught her eye. With a start, she bumped her hip against the counter, causing jar after jar of pickled cabbage to quiver. That was when the cold set itself upon her, in a tight spot at the back of her neck.

Khatijah froze. The porridge still bubbled gently beneath her, and steam still flooded her face, but it stopped feeling warm. It seemed prudent to shout, or move quickly away, but she was too frightened to think of anything else besides standing there, one hand planted firmly on the counter.

Instinctively, she clenched her fingers around the salt grinder. She slid it away from the table, and though she could not say why she chose to do so, she turned her gaze upwards, at the shelf above her. There, the jars had clouded over, some bloodied red, the others opaque white. Her eyes were drawn towards a particular jar in the middle of the rack, whose curtain of white cleared when it had her focus. Inside, a milky-coloured mass curdled upon itself like a clot of grubs, wriggling limbs, she thought, as it rotated in place. From the centre of this clot, wrinkles unfurled like a flower, until, in the depths of its heart, it flicked open an eye.

She drew back, and threw the grinder at the shelf.

In that same instant, she bowed, squealing as she covered her head.

She expected a ghastly sound, like the smash of breaking glass. Instead, there were only the muted whispers of simmering porridge, and not even the whirr of a mosquito to break the mood. Her hand still gripped the salt grinder, which seemed as solid and stalwart as ever. When she finally looked up, instead of fist-sized pickles all over the place, there were only the cooking implements she'd placed there herself.

The cold spot was gone. Her skin still felt cool, though she was certain the temperature in the room had not changed. She rubbed the back of her neck, willing warmth to return.

"Kat," her grandmother called out. "Isn't dinner ready yet?"

"Almost." Khatijah whipped her head towards the kitchen's entrance, listening for footsteps. When she heard her grandmother's shuffles, she added, "You can sit down if you like. I'll call you when it's ready."

"What are you talking about?" Grandmother Jah waddled into the kitchen, making a beeline for the counter. "If I don't help you, we may starve to death." Gesturing at the condiments, she asked, "Is this ready?"

"Yes—", Khatijah began, reaching out to stop her grandmother from troubling herself, then held back. With a grimace, she said, "Let's take that to the table. I'll scoop out the porridge."

"Are you sure you're alright?" the elder woman asked, peering intently at her face. "You look pale."

"I'm fine. Don't worry. I'll get the porridge out."

Her grandmother huffed, and handed the condiments to Khatijah. "Here, you take these to the table. I'll serve the porridge."

"I can do it."

"You don't have to."

Khatijah stared at the salted eggs on the plate she was handed, the yolks as red as the blood she saw in the jars, and the chopped pickles, which she now had no appetite to even consider.

"What are you waiting for?"

She started a smile for her grandmother's benefit, ready to look her in the eye and shrug it all away. The smile died before she could even curl her lips. The kitchen shelf towering behind her grandmother was rattling with growing ferocity as she watched. She let go of the plate she carried.

Grabbing her grandmother by the arm, she used all her strength to shove her away.

"What are you doing?" her grandmother screeched, as the shelf collapsed, smashing crockery and jars against the edge of the counter. The top half slid forward and dangled off a corner of the stove. Grandmother Jah held onto her granddaughter's shoulders when that corner gave, her fingers digging into Khatijah's flesh until it was pinched blue.

When both women dared to survey the remains, they picked their way carefully across the floor, gingerly stepping around porcelain and porridge. Khatijah made sure her grandmother was unhurt before she checked herself for wounds.

"That shelf has been standing there since I was married." Her grandmother lifted a splinter of wood out of the pot, squinting suspiciously at the wall. "I don't believe in old nails. I helped build this house myself, and it was built to last."

"We can visit a store in the morning. Loong and I could find another shelf."

"If you like," her grandmother replied. "Something heavy, maybe, which we can push against the wall."

"Yes," Khatijah added. "Something like that."

"Something that can't be meddled with," muttered Grandmother Jah, as she pried a cup loose from under the counter and inspected it for cracks.

"I can help you clean," Khatijah said, bending down to gather the larger fragments of glass she could see.

Her grandmother laid the cup down, wiped her hand on a rag by the sink, and ruffled her granddaughter's hair. "You should go outside. I'll clean up."

"I can help. Look, the glass will be hard for you to see."

"Kat." Grandmother Jah's voice brooked no dissent. Khatijah saw the hardness in her face, the way her grandmother appeared to be just holding back her anger. "This is none of your concern," Grandmother Jah said. "Go watch TV."

Khatijah dumped the pieces she'd picked up into the sink. "You'll be all right, won't you?"

"I'll be fine." Her grandmother waved her off, raising her voice a decibel or three. "She is dead. No devil woman gets the better of me."

"If we need to call the bomoh—"

"*She* is the least of our worries." Grandmother Jah chanted this at the walls as much as she spoke the words to her granddaughter. "*She* is of no concern to us."

Khatijah gave Grandmother Jah one last look, and nodded. "I'll be outside if you need me."

As she walked into the hall, she heard her grandmother put things back into their place, declaring aloud her intent that these things, and only these things, were welcome in her home. Once she got into that mood, she stayed that way for a while. Khatijah knew better than to interfere.

———

The living room was cool from the air that wafted through the grille. It was a pleasant coolness, like a damp cloth passing over her skin. She sat on the sofa, where the threadbare cushions sank until she could feel the ridges of the rattan frame beneath them, and stared at the TV. The latest police drama from Hong Kong was playing. Her eyes caught the subtitles floating across the screen, but her mind failed to follow the text.

Instead, she looked past the television towards the locked door that led to her Uncle Rahim's childhood bedroom and the slip of white paper pasted atop its door frame.

To the slit under the door she called, quietly, *"Peace be upon you."*

At first, there was nothing. She began to feel silly talking to an empty room. Then, she heard the very faint shuffling of feet, and the tiniest scrapes as they rubbed against the door.

"Grandfather," she whispered, "are you there?"

Khatijah strained to listen for more noises beyond the door, turning the TV's volume down a notch. She couldn't turn it off, for fear of rousing her grandmother's suspicions.

She began whispering urgently. "It was you who did that in the kitchen, wasn't it? I don't know how you did it, but you're the only person who could. Grandmother Aisya doesn't have the heart to do these things.

"Uncle Rahim told me about what you did to him too."

The sound of flying ants, knocking against the light overhead, mimicked the faint bumps she heard against the door. They seemed insistent, but not in any purposeful way, while the TV flooded the space with Cantonese voices, filling the air with boisterous chatter that was at odds with everything else.

"I don't think you care about what you did." Khatijah leaned forward, chuckling bitterly. "Maybe you don't even remember why you do these things to us.

"You're still angry, aren't you? That's why you take it out on Grandmother."

As an afterthought, she added, "I suppose you take it out on Grandmother Aisya too."

She ran her hands through her hair, and turned towards the

darkness beyond the front grille, where the light spilling out of the living room only weakly traversed its borders, highlighting mottled concrete and the broken shadows of bars.

Khatijah couldn't tell if there was anything in the garden just then. She had a feeling the presence there never really left, that Grandmother Aisya's ghost waxed and waned with her mood. What she did feel though, was the silence, a deathly shroud of dusk devoid of even crickets and the normal night-time things that made growing spaces alive.

She shook her head, still clutching and fingering her fringe in reflex. "Someone has to be responsible for this. Someone has to go."

She stared for a long time at the black, rectangular space beneath the bedroom door. The flying ants hummed as they tried in vain to reach the light, their bodies tapping against its plastic casing. To them, the way forward must've seemed so clear, and its boundary so sudden and unseeable. But there were no sounds of shuffling feet, neither heading towards her nor away from her.

Khatijah got up and walked towards the door. Its handle was icy to the touch. She kept her hand firmly gripped around it, until it developed a patina of warmth. And then she drew back, letting her hand fall softly to her side.

"I was there," she said. "I saw what you did. I even ran away from it. You killed Uncle Salih. They only told me the three of you were dead, but it isn't hard to guess you killed her too. Grandmother is right. You're too dangerous to let loose."

As she told him so, a different thought occurred to her. "But then again, if you can't get out," Khatijah began, "and Grandmother Aisya is too weak to do these things . . .

"What if it wasn't you at all?"

She let the thought hang in the air, and poked the doorknob again with a finger. It had returned to being cold. "I guess there's only one person to ask."

The next morning, Khatijah got up for dawn prayers with Grandmother Jah, which helped fortify her resolve. After that, Grandmother Jah watched morning talk shows on TV, one of the many rituals she still adhered to.

Khatijah excused herself with a textbook and headed for the dining area, on the pretext of studying while the day was still fresh. Making sure her grandmother was engrossed with the events on screen, she snuck out through the kitchen door and crept up the path towards the swings.

Mosquitoes hung in the air between overgrown blades of grass. They threw themselves at her in pinpricks of feather-light wings, and her hands were soon bloody from slapping them against her legs.

Dew nestled amongst the moss-eaten tree stumps, little pools for the lizards that scuttled between the roots to drink from. Far away, a neighbour's cockerel crowed. The dawn was still a faint orange band on the horizon. As the sun rose, the rich, black earth would crust over on top, the lizards would hide in their hollows, the mosquitoes would disperse before the light, and even the cockerel would give up. The garden only revolved around itself—a *samsara* stuck at decay.

Grandmother Aisya was waiting on the swings, her face cupped in her hands. Her prayer clothes were wrapped around her in a sheath of spotless white, while her bare feet rested on the ground. Her soles were clean, as though they had been washed for worship. Framed by the glistening tree stumps all around her, basking in the preternatural glow of sunrise, she looked as young as ever.

Khatijah sat beside her on the swings, which she held still by the balls of her feet. "*Peace be upon you,* Grandmother Aisya."

The ghost, as always, did not acknowledge her presence, much less respond to the greeting.

Khatijah pressed on, willing herself to look at where Grandmother Aisya's face would be behind her hands.

"Grandmother Aisya," she asked, "do you remember when Uncle Salih was born?"

Her grandmother grew very still.

Emboldened by what she saw as a tentative connection to this woman, she pressed on, "A child is a grand thing, the culmination of God's great design."

Grandmother Aisya lifted her head. Though she had been crying for months, since they locked Grandfather away, her eyes were bright and clear. Indeed, Khatijah thought she looked far more beautiful than she had been while alive.

Khatijah smiled as gently as she could and softened her voice. "When I delivered him, I said, 'Look, what a beautiful boy he is!'"

The ghost seemed to consider this memory gravely. With a sudden gasp, she turned away to look at her arms, once empty, which now cradled a bundle wrapped in the same white cloth as her clothes. The bundle stayed deathly still. Grandmother Aisya almost immediately began rocking it against her chest, mumbling broken notes that wouldn't quite string together a lullaby. The face that had only a moment ago been so sad now broke into a beatific smile.

But Khatijah grew serious as she continued, "You laughed

and praised God when I told you. But when I brought him to you, you turned away and cried."

"I called him Salih," Grandmother Aisya interjected, stroking the swaddling clothes with her thumb. "It was meant to keep him safe."

"Then you should love him," Khatijah urged. "A mother's love will keep him from harm."

The ghost of Grandmother Aisya fussed over the child in her arms. She inched her hands over a slit in the folds, and ever so slightly, began to pull the cloth apart.

From under it emerged a face, a lump of flesh tinged with grey hairs, covered in the greasy wax of its own afterbirth.

The child that would have been Uncle Salih jerked at his mother's touch. Grandmother Aisya continued caressing his face, running a fingernail over the bloated lid of his one closed eye. At his mother's encouragement, it opened, showing a watery black orb, with only the hints of whites at the edges.

The infant beheld his mother for the first time, and saw tears of flame fall from her cheeks. Together, mother and child burst into a pillar of fire, as red as the sun that was filling the sky above the roof of the house.

Khatijah held up her arms to cover her face, but when she felt no heat, she lowered them slightly, watching transfixed as the pure white cloth blackened, burning only inches away from her. It burned clean, leaving no trace of ash or smoke. There was no smell, nor was there the crackle of a fire, just the image of a flame that burned until nothing was left.

She touched the seat where her grandmother had been. It was still cool to the touch. Softly, under her breath, she whispered, "*And upon you be the peace.*"

From Uncle Rahim's bedroom window, she spied the figure of a man staring pointedly at her. Though his features were a blur, she knew he was angry.

Overhead, on the zinc eaves of the bedroom roof, a large bird flapped down to roost. Between what must have once been its magnificent crop of black feathers, she spied splotches of mangy, bare skin. It was a large, feral cockerel, making guttural calls to the dawn. It glared fiercely at her too, though not with hate. It was a creature that had learned the freedom of the wild, and it had returned to claim its home.

Grandmother Jah, she figured, would turn it into soup if she knew.

Khatijah stole back into the house, leaving the kitchen door open behind her, with the grille locked across the threshold. There would be mosquitoes, but there would also be the cool morning air to go with them. She propped her textbook open on the dining table, ready to appear busy if her grandmother asked. Heading towards the cooking area, she grabbed the kettle from the salvaged cookware Grandmother Jah had piled in a corner and put the water to boil.

Grandmother Jah needed coffee, and the morning needed starting anew. Someone had to be responsible, after all.

Ghani II

"Verily We created Man from a drop of mingled sperm, in order to try him: So We gave him (the gifts), of Hearing and Sight."
—Surah Al Insān, Ayat 2

—

TRAIN STATIONS WERE THE CISTERNS OF SOCIAL INTERACTIONS. THE crowd clustered heaviest at Masjid Jamek, heeding the muezzin's call. On Friday afternoons, men jostled on the LRT towards Jamek Mosque for communal prayers. In their white head wrappings and skullcaps, the pious were differentiated by their excessive love of cloth. Their layered robes, in silky polyester, betrayed their discomfort in patches of damp. The resultant body odour was masked by liberal dashes of rose attar, but the warmth of the omnipresent sun made the overall effect worse.

Packed around them were the office workers, who donned a

songkok and carried a prayer mat for two hours every week, only to tuck these away in a desk drawer or a backpack at the end of the day.

On the other side of the tracks, headed for KL City Central, were the womenfolk. They gathered like an aviary of colour, taking advantage of the extended lunch break to shop and rest. Among them were the youth, some very nearly undressed. Ghani pitied them on behalf of their parents. Children were the shields of their parents in Hell, but neither their cell phones nor their PDAs would shield them while they remained alive. There was no excuse for bad parenting, even a lack of time. Sound morals were about respect established at the root, particularly respect for the Book.

The station echoed with collective chatter, rising from a body with a thousand limbs. A fresh train dumped another load of passengers into the throng—young people from the suburbs. From the other side of the tracks, Ghani noted couples holding hands and leaning into each other's shoulders. The LRT stations ran a series of photographs of such couples near their ticketing booths. Each photo came clearly labelled with the whys and why-nots. In spite of that, or perhaps to spite it, children took advantage of the crowds to be indiscrete.

A lanky couple stumbled in high boots and loose singlets. The girl had her head shaved clean like a convict. The boy had shaved everything but a line through the middle of his own. His bony arm curled low around her waist, and her gaunt hand clung halfway up his back. Light caught metal spots on the boy's face when he turned to whisper something in her ear. The girl tilted her face to his. She was round-cheeked and round-eyed, like a doll.

The next train rushed past like a yellow streak before Ghani's eyes. Whatever he thought he saw, he lost it when his view cleared.

———

Ghani found the mouse at dawn, by the steps of the hen house. It lay open like a blood stain, the intestines, or what remained of them, minced among the broken ribs. Mice died all the time in the garden, sometimes by his hand. But he'd have to talk with the neighbour about his cat, supposing it had taken to stalking his chickens.

He let the chickens out to feed and checked on the crops. The bittergourds were pale green, good for lunch. The mangoes were at various stages of ripening, fire ants festering on the bark in trails of rusty tears. From down the road came the hum and rattle of a car, making its way at parade speed. Ghani reached the front gate in time to watch it pull up. A tall young man with eyes like bright river pebbles and ink-black curls lunged out and immediately wrapped Ghani in his lean arms. "Dad!"

"Rahim." Ghani returned the embrace. "How have you been?"

"Well. I've been well. It's so good to be back."

Ghani stood back to take in the sight of his son, who was a younger version of his own image, stronger and perhaps a little more athletic than Ghani remembered himself to be. Rahim went to help the taxi driver unload his baggage, and another man stepped out of the car. He was small, almost squirrelly, with an evasive nod and a shy smile. Rahim dragged this person before his father. "I'd like you to meet Habib."

"Mr Abdul Rahman, it's a pleasure to meet you, sir." Habib had a weak grip to his salam, but he was softly-spoken, with a natural downtrend to his tone that made everything he said seem that much more polite.

Rahim continued his introduction, "Habib is a good friend of mine. I met him in Perth when he visited my restaurant. His mother was Malaysian. This is his first time here."

"I hope you have a good time in our country, then." Ghani swept his arm towards his house. "Please make yourself at home." As they walked down the garden path, Habib took up the bags Rahim couldn't. A very polite young man, noted Ghani. "Where are you staying?"

"I have a room at the Dynasty downtown. But as Rahim said, I've never been to Malaysia before, so I'm pretty dependent on him to guide me around. It's very kind of you to welcome me." Habib spoke with the slightest twang, though his Malay was clear enough to the native ear.

They were met by Aisya at the front door, very pregnant in her purple dress, even with the drape of her headscarf to hide most of the bulk. The cream scarf made her pale skin shine, and brought out the fine hairs at the edge of her eyebrows, so that they appeared to widen her eyes. She embraced Rahim wearing her gentlest smile. "It's good to have you back. Come in. I've prepared breakfast for three, but it seems we have a guest."

"I hope I haven't troubled you," began Habib.

Rahim cut him short. "I'll help her prepare another place at the table. It's no trouble at all."

Aisya set the table in the garden, so they could have tea among the bougainvilleas, whose flowers today seemed inordinately bright. There was beehive cake, layered cake and of course the rose tea with its amber red swirls in hot water.

"I see you have some very old mango trees, Mr Abdul Rahman." Habib looked up into the canopy and squinted as a sunspot hit his skin.

"They're as old as Rahim. I planted them when he was born." Ghani pointed to a bent branch directly behind the swings. "Some of the mangoes will be ready much earlier this year. The ones on this tree should ripen soon. Do you like mangoes?"

"Oh, yes. Very much, thank you." Habib nodded enthusiastically. "They're so hard to grow where I come from."

Rahim set his cup down with a clatter that seemed slightly too loud. "How long before Youngest Brother is born?"

Aisya clutched her belly and leaned towards her husband, who reached in to grasp her hand. "He'll be born within two weeks, God willing. We think by the seventeenth."

"Have you decided on a name?" Rahim poured his friend more tea, and took care to refill his father's cup as well.

"Salih." Aisya glowed a soft pink as she said so. "I chose that name because it will keep him safe."

———

Habib turned out to be the son of a beef exporter. His family migrated when he was a small child. Now, he was a computer graduate, working with Citibank in Sydney. As Rahim explained over lunch, they'd met when Habib was visiting his parents in Perth, and had been friends ever since. The hours skipped past on dizzy legs that day, for Ghani found the lightness in his heart only increased with the company of his firstborn son.

Khatijah arrived in the evening, as she was wont to do, with her pink headscarf tucked around the edges of her face and under her chin, and her matching skirt almost tripping over her toes. Habib and Rahim sat on the swings. Khatijah stood by, rocking herself on the balls of her feet to the rhythm of their swaying seats. "When will you see Grandmother, Eldest Uncle?"

"Tomorrow. I'll be seeing Big Sister too." Rahim replied. "I hope Mum doesn't mind me coming here first."

"Has she been well?" Ghani glanced politely at his granddaughter, who responded in good cheer.

"Grandmother has been very well."

Ghani saw too much of his first wife's face in Khatijah as she said this. Her smile was warm, but the memory of the other woman left him cold. "How is your mother?"

"Mummy is fine."

"This is good," said Ghani, stepping back.

Habib gave Rahim a puzzled glance, but smiled gently at Ghani when he faced him.

Khatijah looked away from her grandfather to her uncle, who winked and spread his arms wide.

He asked, "Is your mother still so big?"

Khatijah grinned and bobbed her head. "She is! But she won't admit it."

There was laughter again, until a scream roused them to their feet. Ghani rushed into the kitchen, where his wife was huddled into a corner beside the lit stove. A small grey bulge streaked over Ghani's feet as he crossed the threshold, headed determinedly for the chicken pen. It quickly scuttled out of view. Ghani lent his wife his arm, as his son and his guest also entered the kitchen. "It was just a mouse," he began, but Khatijah interrupted.

"Look, Grandfather. The chickens are fighting the mouse."

And true enough, in the chicken run, Ghani's brown hens were attacking the helpless rodent like feral birds, slashing and pecking the fur from its bones. Khatijah ran in to scare them apart, but the effort came too late. The mouse lay on its side, an eye stabbed clean of its socket. The neck was nearly broken off its body, and the tail could not be found.

"They were defending their territory," said Ghani. "That's all it was."

Fatimah

"Thus extinction and natural selection will, as we have seen, go hand in hand."
—*Charles Darwin, The Origin of Species*

———

FATIMAH SAT ON ONE HAND TO KEEP IT WARM, WHILE THE other hand clicked at her phone. Every three minutes and forty-five seconds, the child across the aisle launched into a sharp wail. The timer she played on the screen said so.

He was about five years old. His parents had jammed his arms into the pram's folds and strapped him back so he couldn't hurt himself. From beneath his oversized shorts, his legs hung loose over the edge, thin as broom handles. Even though Fatimah was sure he'd never walk, he was starting to outgrow his pram. Someday soon, they'd have to put him in a wheelchair.

His skin was pale, as white as the Taiwanese actresses on the six o'clock soap operas, and just as smooth. His large irises were so dark, they seemed to absorb the fluorescent lighting. When he stopped to catch his breath, the child stared at the world from beneath those eyes, framed with thick, dusky eyelashes. But the fact that he stared so much meant little, because it was clear he registered none of it.

There seemed no particular reason for his wailing, which sounded partly like a demand for attention and partly like a shout of pain. His parents, absorbed in their magazines about immaculately trimmed gardens and even better living rooms, ignored him. If a child cried that often and that regularly, what was the point of paying him any mind?

Fatimah pitied them. No parent with the right means brought such a child into this world. Yet this child, deformed as he was, clearly had people who cared for him. It wasn't that his parents failed to love him when they ignored his pleas. Instead, they had simply become accustomed to their fate. Still, she wondered what they were doing here so late. Official visiting hours ended two hours ago. Even a normal child would be in bed this close to midnight. Perhaps, they too had a dying grandmother waiting, and this was the only heir they could produce before their ancestor drew her last breath.

The hospital was cold. Sitting in its vast hall chilled her to the bone. The air conditioning flowed across her shoulders, slipping its fingers down her back and over her knuckles. She wished she'd brought a shawl, just for the extra warmth. Fatimah breathed in the smell of soap that permeated the place, which threatened to saturate her hair and every pore of her skin, so much so that she wanted to run home and scrub it off. A part of her wanted to know what the smell was hiding, if it was trying to hide something bad with something worse.

Fatimah's husband, Malik, left earlier. Someone needed to mind the house, and he was only an in-law, after all.

Her mother was in here somewhere. Fatimah had yet to see her. The doctors dropped words like 'stroke' and 'fragile' when they explained what went wrong, but nothing about when she could see her. This was why Fatimah rushed to this cold, unnaturally bright place, where the fluorescence stamped out depth and shadow.

It was bad enough her mother returned to that house. But exorcists? Her dead father rising from his grave? Her mother had to be losing her mind.

She deserved to spend her retirement in the care of her children, in a cosy, safe house where she could enjoy the company of her grandkids. She deserved better—and Fatimah worried she might not live to have that chance.

As she worried, she fidgeted, sliding uncomfortably on her plastic seat. Corridors emanated from each corner of the waiting area, eerily silent passages from which could be heard the occasional squeak of wheels. Nurses strode determinedly between their stations, before disappearing around corners. Doctors in white coats were a somewhat rarer sight, but they too sailed through this pastel space, billowing past like a cloud of deliberate restraint.

At the far end of the seats, near the corner that eventually led to the entrance, sat a wooden counter—the reception desk—now abandoned after office hours. The signs overhead were plain white placards hanging from slender chains: "Check-in", "Check-out" and "Payments".

Her daughter, Khatijah, rounded the corner closest to "Check-in". She carried a plastic bag, from which protruded bottles of mineral water and the rolled edge of a newspaper. As she walked up, she smiled to Fatimah, and pulled out one of the bottles. "The petrol station was far away, but there was a curry house nearby. I wanted to get us some tea, but they only sold it in plastic bags. I was afraid it was too messy to bring here."

Fatimah reached out for the bottle with a nod. "Water's fine."

"Are you hungry? I got us some nuts."

Her mother shook her head. "No. It's late, but this is still a hospital. If you're hungry, you can go back to the curry house and have something to eat. I can give you money."

Khatijah stuffed the packet of nuts she'd bought back into the plastic bag. She took out a smaller box of mints instead. "Want one?"

Again, Fatimah declined.

"I'm not hungry," Khatijah said, "Just peckish." She twisted the wrapper off and popped a sweet into her mouth. In profile, she strongly resembled her grandmother, with her flat nose and round, full cheeks. Her burnished skin was too dark to be beautiful, though it was smooth and showed no signs of the pimples girls got at her age. She exuded her grandmother's natural confidence even in repose—the kind that Fatimah believed a nice boy might one day find unthreatening. Seeing her made Fatimah feel slightly sad, but also slightly proud, knowing her mother's legacy extended to this child.

Khatijah's mass of black curls surrounded her small face. It was at the length where it was just starting to brush uncomfortably against her cheek, and Khatijah had a tendency to push her hair back behind her ears whenever she bent her head forward, as she did now. When another cry rose from the child beside them, she angled her head briefly and politely towards him.

The screen of Fatimah's phone glowed, buzzing gently in her hand. An SMS arrived from Rahim.

"Your uncle sent me a message," said Fatimah. "He's arriving on Friday."

"I can pick him up from the airport."

"We'll figure it out on the day itself. He's arriving in the morning; you might need to be in school."

Khatijah blanched at her mother's response. "Grandmother's more important."

"She is, but your father and I can handle your uncle."

"Does he know where he's staying?"

"He can stay with us if he has to. We have room."

"He can stay with me at Grandmother's house."

"You're staying with us in the meantime, and Rahim won't be staying at your grandfather's house either."

"But—"

"We can give him Mother's room. You can sleep in your own. There's always place for everyone." Fatimah caught her daughter's insolent look and returned it with one of equal stubbornness. "You are not arguing with me over this." And to herself she added, *That house has caused enough trouble for us.*

"All my books are at Grandmother's house."

"We'll swing by there in the morning. We'll have to get her things anyway."

Turning pointedly back to her phone, Fatimah quickly stabbed away her response to Rahim. The time in Perth corresponded with the time in Kuala Lumpur. Fatimah felt bad about messaging her brother that late, but everything she could tell him was another worry she could take off his mind.

He had been kind enough to clear the old house when their father died, the fate she had been too angry to face. She offered to hire a cleaning agency so he wouldn't have to do it, but Rahim ultimately gave the situation more dignity than she knew she could muster. The temptation to burn all *that woman's* things would have been too much, for a start.

Beside her, Khatijah was reading the World section of her newspaper, refusing to make eye contact.

A nurse in an electric blue uniform crossed the hall towards them. She was dark-skinned, in that richly polished veneer that marked her as a foreign Indian rather than a local one. Hospitals private and otherwise were filled with them. The locals had no drive to care for their own countrymen. She gave the nurse and the family across the aisle quizzical looks.

This time, when the child began to cry, his mother reached out to shush him, making sure to give the nurse an embarrassed smile as she did so. The child let out a hearty gurgle, apparently pleased to have an audience.

The nurse, whose tag read "Reja", addressed the woman attending to her son. "Mrs. Lee?" she asked, her accent keening with high pitched 'E's.

"My mother. I'm her daughter and this is my husband," the woman replied, pointing to the man beside her.

"Madam," the nurse continued, "Mrs Lee is ready to see you now." She waved a hand at the child, smiling, "Children are not allowed into her ward."

"That's alright, Prita. I'll stay here," said the father, gently tugging the pram towards him.

Prita gathered her things, kissing her son on the forehead before she left, with the nurse leading the way.

The child seemed to follow her path until they rounded the corner and disappeared. She thought he would start crying again, but he preoccupied himself with gurgling instead. His father arranged his magazine neatly on his lap and resumed reading.

Nurse Reja bustled back five minutes later. "Mrs Ghani?"

"That's me," answered Fatimah.

"Your mother is ready to see you now."

Fatimah turned to Khatijah, who was already folding her newspaper back into her bag. "I'm going with you," she said.

"Would that be all right?" Fatimah asked the nurse.

Nurse Reja replied, "That is all right, Madam. We just have to be quiet."

They followed the nurse through a side corridor into an octagonal space with a tapering glass atrium at the very top. The floors above looked down on the ground level from thick wooden banisters. On their floor, a bank of three lifts took up an entire wall. Nurse Reja summoned one in quick order and ushered them inside.

Fatimah was glad for the nurse's efficiency. She was even more relieved when the lift did not stop anywhere before their destination.

The nurse, their guide through this relentlessly white rat maze, walked calmly and with dignity, taking only the minimal amount of steps required to steer them towards the right room. Its door was slightly ajar by virtue of a rubber stopper attached to its foot. She opened and held the door for them. "Your mother is sleeping," she said. "She's not in any discomfort right now, though you should let her rest. If you need anything, please use the button by the bed." Then she left them with a polite nod, letting the door close gently behind her.

What was it about hospital beds that made anyone in them seem so much smaller than they should be? Fatimah remembered—and oh, God, there she went, 'remembered', as if her mother weren't even here—that her mother had been a robust, vital woman, not this sunken, brittle person in a cotton gown. But her face couldn't lie, this face that looked like her own and her daughter's too. It was her mother on that bed, her close-cropped curls darkened from damp, the forehead barely glistening in the palest glow of an overhead light. It was her hand that Fatimah grasped, worn enough that she could feel the bones clearly through the skin, and not remember a time when that hand felt so *thin*.

Khatijah pressed close beside her, resting her hands upon the side of the bed, the plastic bag gone. The look on her child's face was solemn. Neither of them knew what to say. Finally, Khatijah cupped her hands in supplication and recited a prayer.

Fatimah cupped her hands in turn, adding to her daughter's words. "O Allah! We ask you to bless our beloved mother and grandmother who is sick. Grant us strength and wisdom in these difficult times. Bless us with your mercy and healing. Amen."

"Amen."

"Thank God for small mercies," said Fatimah. "She's asleep and isn't feeling any pain."

Khatijah reached over to tuck her grandmother's blanket in. "She's just sleeping," she said. "Maybe she'll wake up in the morning."

"Maybe." Fatimah continued stroking her mother's knuckles, still amazed at how fleshless each finger felt. She whispered, "I'd like to hold her hand a bit more."

"Then maybe we'll do that," replied Khatijah, smoothing down the blanket one last time before crossing to the chair where she'd put her bag.

Fatimah had been so intent on seeing her mother, she hadn't even noticed there were chairs in the room. She carried one over. Its skinny metal legs wobbled when she sat down. The thin curve of plastic that formed the seat didn't feel like it should hold her weight even though it could. Like all things about this hospital experience, it felt fragile and ephemeral. By design, the act of being in a hospital was about minimising how long you stayed. The shortest visit was always the best outcome.

Fatimah was resigned to lingering here for tonight, but she would still hate every minute of it. To pass the time, she thought about the story she should tell her mother while she slept. She thought about Khatijah, reading her newspaper close by, and how much of herself was in her child, and through her, her grandmother as well. It was as though each generation of women had refined itself further until here was the jewel she raised, which she brought before her own mother.

That, she believed, was what she would murmur into her mother's ear—as out of earshot to her daughter as she could manage. They couldn't let the pride get to Khatijah's head.

———

In the morning, Malik arrived with hot tea and packets of rice for breakfast. He would take over watching Mum while they went home to shower, and if anything changed, he would call. Neither Fatimah nor Khatijah felt tired.

Her mother had not awakened, in spite of what the nurse said.

Fatimah had not returned to her childhood home for the longest time, and almost refused to now. But she'd said they would swing by for her daughter's things, before they returned to their family's real home.

The village she'd remembered had grown into a township. The drive through it was a serpentine weave that quickly devolved from a single tarred lane to rivers of packed red dust. More frightening than trying to stay on the road and not swerve into a fencepost was the fear that she might see someone who recognised her, some aged neighbour whose first instinct was to ululate her name and summon relatives to gawk.

Few things thrived on the thick, water-resistant clay. The dark green foliage behind each chicken wire fence was the work of decades of careful tending, each proud gardener bringing to life the fruit trees that would grow with his children. Muscular, wiry chickens on legs built for running dashed across the narrow lanes and under the gaps in people's gates. Their car passed occasional strangers, mostly young people born after her time, who wandered the village with sullen expressions on their faces, though not annoyance directed at her that she could tell.

Houses rose around them on concrete stilts, half-hidden behind trees and thick black cables strung between wooden telephone poles. Ditches and monsoon drains criss-crossed the whole village even when she was a child, but it was a given that if it rained, it would flood. Modern embellishments peeped out from treetops, a blue flag with white scales for the ruling political party, or a faded green flag with a white circle for its opposition next door. Every few lots, there was a shiny new car in the driveway and a satellite dish mounted prominently on the eave of the home's twenty-year-old zinc roof.

As they approached the residence where the village chief once lived, the lanes again widened into tarred roads. The chief's roof, sparkling with brand new red tiles, still towered over its neighbours. It was the first fully concrete and brick structure erected in the village. *Government money*, people whispered at the time. The only other thing built to such modern standards was the mosque.

Her father's house stood away from the village, divided by a wide drain from the road behind the chief's house. Father owned a large piece of land, and both her parents had preferred to seclude themselves on it.

Fatimah approached the house with even more apprehension than she had the village. The sharpened spindles of dead bushes jutted through the fence like barbed wire. She heard the thorns dig into her car as she slowed before the gates.

Damn it," she said, pulling on the handbrake. Whacking both palms against the steering wheel in frustration, she heard her daughter unclip her seatbelt beside her.

"I'll unlock the gate" Khatijah said, halfway out.

Fatimah backed the car away from the dead bougainvillea. The sound of its retreating fingers, echoing along the driver's side, made her wince.

Khatijah held the gate open as she drove in, leaving it to swing back as she jogged to the front door.

The low zinc roof, bearing down upon the weather-beaten walls of her childhood home, seemed almost to notice her and frown. The window of the bedroom where she and later Rahim used to sleep was an impassable rectangle of slatted glass, covered over with a wrought iron grille that itself looked like the dead vines of something horrible, and peculiarly, seemed to grow even darker and more unwelcoming the closer she pulled up the driveway.

Khatijah's car, the small, white indulgence from her father, was parked neatly between the window and the swings.

Rahim had warned Fatimah about the mango trees, whose disappearance became apparent when she was able to peer over Khatijah's car. Their stubs covered the place where an orchard once stood, eaten smooth by moss and forested with healthy, adult weeds that waved full heads of burrs in a light breeze. Bugs dodged about over the teeming mass of undergrowth. Grey, brittle branches, still hanging onto life in patches of yellowing leaves and papery petals of faded reds and purples, bordered the whole garden. The only clear space left was under the swings, where scuffling feet wore down any grass before it could grow.

When Fatimah got out, she immediately checked for damage. The scratches ran as deep as the awful sound they'd made, making five broken lines from the side mirror to the handle, their ragged path edged with fine silvery powder.

The sight of the scratches seemed to mock her for even coming here.

Khatijah came over to look, running a finger along a line of metal dust. "Those are bad," she said, adding nothing to improve Fatimah's mood.

"Let's get into the house," Fatimah replied, wanting to put distance between herself and her shame.

As she headed towards the front door, she once again caught sight of the window to the children's old bedroom. The grille glinted unnaturally over the blackened glass, like the living tendrils of some horrid beast rising to possess the house. Taken aback, she reached out to touch the metal leaves, to see if they were as animated as they looked. The slender grooves were incredibly cold where she expected wetness but were indeed metal. Her fingertips came back stained with red.

Over the threshold, the house appeared only in minor disarray. There were shoe prints on the living room floor, likely from the rescue workers who'd taken her mother to the hospital. The path to the master bedroom was relatively clear, so there was little to get in their way. Fatimah noted the cobwebs in the corners, between—and though she couldn't see it, probably behind—the TV shelf, and in the corners of the room. Since Khatijah was not the best housekeeper, she figured her mother simply skipped the corners she was no longer able to reach.

The air hung low, weighing down upon her shoulders in an invisible shroud. The floor felt sticky against her bare feet from the moment she took off her shoes. Instead of the cooling comfort that should have met her soles, the tiles were clammy, like the skin on a fevered forehead. The stench of must, filled with the sour notes of old paper and moulding cornices, grew stronger as she crossed the room. It reached a head as they passed the children's old bedroom, where the rot mixed with the very faint hint of roach.

Charging through the kitchen, Fatimah opened the windows that faced the weed-ridden yard and the backdoor, making sure the grille that covered it was locked shut. She would make coffee, except she preferred having coffee in her own home, eschewing the hospitality of a stranger's resting place. Had she truly intended to stay here for longer than half an hour, she would have worried about mosquitoes arriving with the fresh air, but oxygen was more important in a house whose last resident spent the night at a hospital.

Pacing across the cooking area, she noted that someone had removed the rough-hewn wooden shelves where her mother's prized pickles and old crockery were stacked. Instead, a waist high shelving unit in plasticky laminate held a couple of pickle jars and half the mismatched plates and cups from her child-hood meals. The gleaming white microwave at the corner was probably Rahim's doing.

She ducked her head out of the kitchen doorway and called, "Kat, are you ready yet?"

"Almost," came her daughter's reply.

"We're only picking up things you really need, and a few things for Grandmother. We can get the rest later."

"I know!"

Fatimah exited into the hallway, hoping the sound of her footsteps would hurry the girl up. She moved towards the tele-phone recess, swearing her father hadn't changed the phone in twenty years, and even then probably because the telephone company sent him a new model against his will. When was the last time she'd seen a perfectly rectangular telephone? The receiver, individually numbered buttons and the base were hard plastic, with sharp angles and crisply delineated numer-als. There used to be a much older model in its place, with the kind of dial that one turned with a finger, facilitating long, lazy conversations over crackly copper lines. That was the phone from her years of growing up. This 'new' model arrived when she'd already left and married, possibly even when Khatijah was still a toddler.

In an age when landlines were almost obsolete, she was compelled to pick up the receiver and listen for the dial tone.

The sound that emerged was like a rush of air through the tiny ear holes, as though she had breathed hard into the mouthpiece. Static? She drew back slightly.

It was about then that she realised how cold her legs felt. She put the receiver down to rub her calves, trying to will blood back into her feet.

When she looked up, a slip of white caught her eye. Pasted above the door of the old children's bedroom was a piece of paper, with the name Allah printed in elegant calligraphic script. The bomoh's work no doubt. She knew her mother had also hired a Taoist nun. Did she ward off hopping vampires? Fatimah grasped the door handle firmly, giving it a good shove. The knob was stiff and icy, but gave with a reluctant click.

No wonder the window seemed so dark outside. The room was nearly lightless from dust. It slathered the window in a thick coat of grey and the floor—she couldn't countenance stepping onto that floor. Rahim hadn't even tried to bring a broom in here.

A light, tentative draft flowed over her feet. Fatimah reflexively stomped in place. Had the wind picked up outside? Briefly, she could have sworn the tendrils of dust hanging from the ceiling had moved. The air had to be coming in from somewhere, but there was no way she could see herself crossing the filthy room on bare feet to check the window. Fatimah pulled the door back towards its latch, leaving just enough of a gap that some of its dank air would escape without the dirt.

When she crossed to the kitchen again, Khatijah was there, wrapping a pickle jar with plastic bags.

"Why are you bringing that?" Fatimah asked.

"Grandmother should have porridge when she wakes up. She likes it with this."

"You're bringing that to the hospital?" Fatimah shook her head. "I guess it might help her appetite. We'll get some fish essence before we go back too. It's healthier." She fidgeted with the door as she watched her daughter carefully double wrap the jar, and slowly tie the knots on top. "Are your things packed yet?"

"They're in the bedroom."

"I'll carry them to my car. Don't forget we're bringing your car too." Fatimah strode towards her parents' bedroom, where the bags her daughter had prepared waited on the floor, unzipped, and drawers filled with clothes were left open. She squatted down beside the bags and poked through some of their topmost items, muttering with distaste, "All the things she wants to bring are trash."

She began pulling out clothes from the drawers, things for her mother and things for her daughter, replacing items from each bag and folding away the leavings. Towards the bottom of her mother's headscarves, an edge of blue cloth smudged with ink caught her eye. Like a magician unfurling a string of kerchiefs from his hat, she gently pulled it out. It was a child's primary school uniform. Originally a solid navy blue, the colour on the pinafore had faded almost to a pastel. School uniforms then and now were always made from such cheap cloth, but everyone simply assumed the kids would grow out of them fast. Under the edge of the skirt, she had written her name in marker pen, but like all things, it too bled out. Who kept something so old?

Behind her, she heard Khatijah enter the room and exclaim, "What are you doing?"

"Kat, you have better clothes than these," said Fatimah, briskly sweeping the dress back into the drawer. "and your grandmother needs something a bit warmer."

"I've already packed them."

"You didn't pack them right."

The look on her daughter's face reminded her of herself, at many points throughout her childhood, before school sent her away. Remembering how she reacted to her own mother softened her features. This house was bringing out the worst in everyone.

"Is that for the bag too?" Fatimah asked, gesturing at the plastic bag in Khatijah's hands.

"It's the pickles."

"Put them in the car. On the floor. We don't want it spilling out." As she zipped everything up, she added, "Go close the windows and the kitchen door. I'll carry these."

Khatijah trampled loudly down the hallway, a clear show of annoyance.

The last thing Fatimah needed was to deal with more childish antics. She huffed and hoisted the bags in both hands towards the porch. They were well-filled bags, no space wasted. Might as well bring as much as they could even in this small amount of time. Popping open the car, she hefted the bags in, leaving it unlocked for a quick escape.

Khatijah was taking her time.

From where Fatimah stood, she could see her daughter waiting just beyond the corner that led to the telephone alcove.

Khatijah was staring in the direction of the children's bedroom, her body crouched as though she were ready to spring.

"Kat!" her mother called.

She thought Khatijah glanced her way, but quickly resumed her watch over the bedroom door.

"Kat!" Fatimah called again. "We have to go soon!"

When Khatijah failed to respond, Fatimah walked back into the house. The door she had left ajar had swung back open. The midday sun must have really lit up outside. Even through all the dirt, she could see the outline of shelves and mosquito netting, the latter's bulk an amorphous softness that smothered most of the room. "What are you waiting for?" she asked. "Come on."

Something about Khatijah's face, the shell-shocked expression she wore, the rigid limbs, made her pause. "Kat?" called out Fatimah again. This time, she tried touching her daughter's arm.

Almost immediately, it was clear something was wrong. Khatijah's skin was cold, in fact, the air all around them felt cold, like someone had left an air-conditioner on at full blast. And though she was standing still, Fatimah could feel the light trembling that ran the length of her daughter's body. It was as though she was shivering in place, her lips growing purple.

If the cold had to come from somewhere, it would be the open bedroom. Fatimah quickly grasped the door handle and tried to pull it shut. The door held stiff, like someone was also pulling it from the other side. All her strength refused to make it yield.

Fingers stroked Fatimah's hair.

It was a familiarity that halted any thought, any rational movement. All that remained was concentrating on the sensation, trying to make sure it was real.

But there it was again. A second stroke, gently following her scalp down to her neck.

"Child," came the voice, grave and tender, out of another memory that pervaded this house.

The words, when she turned, came from Khatijah's moving lips, the hand that reached for her hair was Khatijah's hand, but nothing about it was Khatijah.

Fatimah shrieked.

"You!" she screamed, grabbing Khatijah and shaking her shoulders. "Get out of my daughter!"

Khatijah's lips moved again, but her face was blank, no emotion, no expression human or otherwise. "Welcome home," it said.

"Don't you dare call this home," Fatimah warned. "Don't you dare even tell me that."

"We waited," said the voice, "You came back."

"And you can bloody keep waiting," Fatimah spat out. "How dare you even talk to me?"

The hand reached out again for Fatimah's hair. She slapped it away. The face contorted into a smile. The lips said, "I've missed you."

"Don't you dare say that!" Fatimah kept screaming, "You don't deserve to tell me that!

"You abandoned our family.

"You wouldn't even give my mother a divorce.

"You shamed her. You shame me. You don't deserve anyone."

Shadows gathered on the walls, looming fingers that insisted on embracing her even in silhouette, shadows like trees branching everywhere. The afternoon sun flared behind them and only seemed to make the shadows stronger.

Fatimah refused to cry. More than that, she refused to forgive. "This is not my home," she said. "None of us are coming here ever again."

Khatijah loosened her limbs and stumbled. Her mother immediately encircled her in an embrace. A brief quiet followed, before a light patter began picking its way over the ceiling, like chicken feet on a zinc roof.

Fatimah felt, rather than heard, the shiver that ran through her, diving deep into the concrete beneath her feet. There, from the depths of the house's timbers, began a distant roar. Its crescendo rose through the foundations, screaming from the very pores of the walls. Someone had pulled a mandrake by its top. Now it was cursing them to their grave.

She dragged, half-carried Khatijah forward. The river of air that pushed against her was icy, dry and disquieting like the insides of a tomb. It smelled of rot, of sweet composting earth. That essential spirit of its perfume, the scent of spades digging into garden beds and grit against the fingers, was all too familiar. Feeling it running through her hair and touching her skin disgusted her. She rejected this sensation with every fibre of her being.

The furniture around them began to twist into impossible dimensions, rattan liquefying out of shape and wrapping in multiple strands up the wall. Glass burst into silvery splashes of sand. Fatimah expected it to hurt, but it flew over their heads like someone had shot fairy dust out of a cannon. They passed wood taking root on vertical surfaces, digging into plaster. Her hand was red from the rust that squeezed out when she grabbed on vines to move, step after increasingly sticky step. Like in mud, lifting each foot created a vacuum that loudly gulped in air, but it was too slippery, too oddly thin. Only when she finally grasped the edge of the front door frame, her nails peeling up splinters, did she realise she was stepping through oil.

Tiny black scales surged up from her fingertips, speckling her arm and sleeve. She braced herself in order to swing Khatijah forward just a little more. When her daughter lurched forward, she let go and pushed Kat's back with all her might. Khatijah's eyes opened with fear the moment she crossed the threshold. Her arms flew out in front of her to cushion the impact, hold onto the front grille.

"Pull me to you!" Fatimah shouted.

Her daughter flailed out an arm in the direction of her voice, which Fatimah grabbed. Though her eyes wandered feverishly about, like someone woken abruptly from sleep, Khatijah had enough of her senses to keep clinging on.

Together, they shoved against the front grille, coiling their hands and feet in whatever crevices would fit. The vortex pulled at their hair and tried to stick its burrs into their clothes, tried to carry them away with its maddened voice.

Until finally, it stopped.

The two women dared to lift their heads. Stepping off the iron grille, they tumbled onto the porch.

The first thing Fatimah noticed were the black spots on her knuckles and up her sleeves—cockroaches—which she frantically brushed off. Some were already dead, crushed in the escape.

"Look," said Khatijah, as she helped her mother up.

Fatimah turned back, tensing for a fight. What lay before them was a house overgrown. Mould, slick like blood, stained the walls deeply in dark, reddish-green splatters. The floor ran rampant with roots thick as a man's leg, cracking through concrete that seemed as fragile as dry, dead earth. Branches gouged so cleanly through the rooms, they looked as though it was the house, not they, that had been constructed around them. Instead of greenery, the house was crowned with shattered-through zinc sheets, broken into grooved pieces as large as taro leaves.

The light pattering that preceded the carnage started up again overhead. Black-feathered birds, long-necked, bald-headed and with clawed feet landed on the eaves of the house. The creatures stared down at the women with beady, reptilian aloofness. One bird alighted with a rat between its pointed beak, its kill still bloody.

"The chickens," Khatijah declared.

"He can bloody well have them," replied Fatimah. Slowly picking her way to her car, she continued, "Let's go home." Remembering what her mother used to say about speaking your intent so as not to invite bad spirits, she added, "We're returning—to *our* home."

As they drove off in convoy, her daughter's car in front of hers, Fatimah heard a hollow caw. It could have been a child's wail or a crow. The carrion birds feasted on the roof of her father's house, pecking out his eyes and peeling off his scalp. Only the body remained.

Ghani III

THE NEXT DAY, GHANI FED HIS CHICKENS HALF THE USUAL AMOUNT OF *grain, and noted they ate very little of it. The hens rested around their pen and ambled lazily as the warm spots of sun moved across the ground. Ghani found the remains of two more mice in the hen house, and the corpses of a dozen lizards, as well as what could've been the skull of a toad. Aisya had demanded the lot be slaughtered, forbidden as it was to eat the flesh of carnivorous animals. Ghani still believed his chickens were only defending themselves, and refused to discuss the matter further.*

Rahim emerged from the kitchen doorway. "Peace be upon you."

"And upon you be the peace. Did you just wake up?"

"I did."

"Have you had breakfast yet? You should've rested more." Ghani swung the gate of the chicken coop shut, latching it firmly. *His son leaned on the fence surrounding the pen, watching him with dulled eyes.*

"It's alright. I promised I'd have breakfast with Mum."

"You're going to see her this early?"

"I promised."

Ghani frowned. "Will you be there all day?"

Like a younger mirror of his face, his son returned the frown. "No, I'm free after lunch."

"Good. I need to speak with you."

Rahim's expression softened. "What's this about?"

Ghani put away the grain bag and put on his gloves. Each finger slid loosely over his skin, the rubber grips worn down enough that he could almost feel his skin. His pruning shears were sharp, with a beak like a parrot's. "You remember Uncle Hanif from the mosque?"

"Yes."

"I'm going to invite him over for tea. I want you to be there."

"Okay."

"You used to play with his children when you were younger. Do you remember?"

"He had a boy and a girl, didn't he? The girl used to be good friends with Big Sister."

Ghani applied his shears to a dead branch of bougainvillea, the leaves yellowed going into brown. "Muslimah graduated the same year you did. She's now with the Development Bank. Doing quite well there."

Rahim walked behind his father as he snipped at more branches. Ghani could hear him over the crunch of the soft wood. With the presence of his son close by, Ghani continued, "Muslimah is about a year your junior. I've known Hanif almost as long as I've been alive, so our families are practically the same now. He's waiting for his grandchildren too."

Rahim seemed to pause. Other than the shuffle of falling branches, it was quiet.

Ghani pressed on. "I think it'd be good if the two of you could meet. It's been a while since you've seen each other. The people from the mosque keep asking after you."

"I'm sure they would."

Ghani turned to face his son, and saw how his face hardened. "The mosque means a lot to me. It'd be good if we could get closer to them."

Rahim glanced at his watch and nodded. "Well, it's time to head to Mum's."

"Don't forget tea."

"We'll see."

———

"We'll see."

There hadn't been a tea. The evening of that day came and went. Ghani sat in Habib's hotel room, picking at the green and red fleur-de-lis upholstered into the arm of his chair. Rahim sat opposite his father, at the edge of the bed, whereas Habib preferred to stand after serving black coffee from his complimentary bar.

"Where were you?" Ghani strained to see the humility in his son, who gazed at him as though he wasn't there.

"Father," he started, "it would seem there are matters we must address—"

"Stop wasting time. If it is as important as you say, address it."

Rahim cleared his throat, and began again. "Father," he said, "there won't be a marriage from me. Not even one. Not in this lifetime."

"Nonsense," replied Ghani. "It's the responsibility of every sound Muslim man to marry."

"This is true, but –"

"It is a responsibility you cannot avoid," Ghani repeated. He took a sip of Habib's coffee. The boy made horrible coffee, too bitter and too sweet all at once. "Furthermore, you aren't getting any younger."

"This is why I thought we should talk." His son cleared his throat, eliciting a cough from Habib. "Perhaps it's best to understand that I simply can't choose any woman I'd prefer to spend my life with."

"Is it the work?"

"No, it's not the work, though it's true I have a lot of work."

"Then, this is not a problem. If it's a woman you need, there are many ways to ask." Ghani worked with an even tone, noting his son squirming at its application.

"I don't think you understand."

"No, of course I do."

"No, I don't think you do." Rahim looked to Habib, who began to politely stare at his shoes. But his son reached out a hand towards him, and the other man reached out a hand towards Rahim. The scene struck Ghani as being something familiar, out of recent history, as if it were performed by young people in a train station.

Ghani set down his coffee cup, refusing to drink a drop more. Scrubbing the imaginary dust from his pants, he stood with his back straight and his head held high. With his eyes looking at neither man, he addressed them both. "Take your luggage out of my house by tomorrow. Don't bother to return."

By the time he reached home, the chickens had already flown to the roof, their sharpened claws like tiny heels marching over the tiles. The mangoes hung heavy from the trees, like clusters of geriatric breasts. Mosquitoes hummed in their shade, attacking the smallest changes in the air.

Khatijah sat on the swings, rocking herself by the balls of her feet, a bundle wrapped in a pink headscarf in her arms. Her head was shaved bald like a convict, making her round eyes seem wider. As she clutched the bundle closer, she cooed a lullaby. When she noticed him at the gate, she rose full of smiles and praise for God. "Youngest Uncle is born."

Ghani took quick strides to her side, ripping the child from her hands and gazing upon his youngest son in earnest. The child curled in his wraps was pale tinged with blue, bald but for the finest grey hairs upon his head. Staring up at him was a single open unblinking eye. Ghani lifted the child's right ear to his lips, and sang what all good fathers must to the newly born, "Allah is the Greatest. I bear witness that there is no one worthy of worship except He. I bear witness that Muhammad is the Messenger of Allah." *Then, Ghani needed only to regard the thing for a moment more, before dashing its head upon the floor.*

To the messenger he let fly his free palms, beating upon her bare scalp and exposed neck until she screamed into his face and fled. He followed the sound of her slippers clomping against the paved road until it could no longer be heard.

Overhead, his chickens circled the house and feigned swoops, perhaps waiting to pick at the corpse not yet cold on his front porch. The bougainvilleas rose in piles of violet and wine, stretching up from the corners of his garden like tongues of Hell. Overripe mangoes cried fire ants that pooled at the foot of the trees and spilled across the tar-black soil.

Ghani stepped across the threshold into the silence of his home, where things stood still, unlike his garden. Aisya lay sleeping in their bed, small and lithe and well able to bear more children, though at the moment she was unable to hold so much as a whisper. Ghani lay beside her as if in a dream, the memory of a dream of a dark place and the feelings of being un-new. When she lifted her head, he smothered her down. When she spoke, he silenced her with fingers over her tongue. It was like this until, with his neck slumped on her shoulder and her body cold, they were brought before the Garden, upon which they bore witness but could not pass.

————

"From the war of nature, from famine and death, the most exalted object which we are capable of conceiving, namely, the production of higher animals, directly follows."

—*The Origin of Species,* Charles Darwin

About the Author

A.M. MUFFAZ IS A MALAYSIAN WRITER BASED IN SAN FRANCISCO. Her short stories and poetry have previously appeared in magazines on and offline, including *The Dark, ChiZine* and *Fantasy Magazine*. She whiles away her days with a husband who is way too kind as he is tall and a food inspector cat who speaks in pirate. When not reading obsessively difficult books, she is probably thinking about obsessively difficult things. She enjoys history, video games//, anime, manga and cute, fluffy animals. Oh, and murder. Because some murders are clearly more delightful than others. More about her writing can be found at: www.ammuffaz.com

CPSIA information can be obtained
at www.ICGtesting.com
Printed in the USA
FSHW021608160921
84814FS

9 781952 283161